Also by Catherine Gammon

The Martyrs, The Lovers
China Blue
Sorrow
Beauty and the Beast: Stories from the 1970s
Isabel Out of the Rain

The Gunman & the Carnival

for Deb, Deborah, Geri, and Lynn

Contents

Eudora Loved Her Life

EUDORA LOVED HER life. She had been sober three years and nicotine-free for two and a half. She had not quit her necessary day job. She had not stayed involved with an abusive boyfriend. She had made love to a man who became her best friend and never again her lover. Her weight was right, her clothes fit well, she had just turned forty, and the street where she lived was suddenly purple with jacaranda. On turning thirty-five she had been depressed, had felt the approach of darkness and death, much as she had at twenty-one, and that had been with a baby in her arms and a husband at her side. Now her daughter was in school at Stanford and her former husband, a D.C. lobbyist for progressive causes, was filling the gap the financial aid package left. Her own dull job paid well enough to give her the freedom to do the work that mattered to her, and she still had hope for that work to break out of its privacy and fully inhabit public space.

To celebrate her birthday, she took the day off and drove to the beach.

She found a woman there, a body, face down in the sand. Dead, or maybe dead.

She called 911 and waited.

She was alone on the beach. She had chosen a stretch she knew to be isolated, even from runners and dog walkers, likely to be solitary on a morning like this one, overcast and cold.

She wondered whether to wait. She wondered what had happened to the woman and sat in the sand beside her. She didn't dare touch her. She didn't know if her touch might bring harm, to the woman or to herself. She looked at the woman's hair, splayed out dark and damp, her face hidden.

The woman's body and clothes suggested she was young. Younger than Eudora. Her pale skin was tattooed, ornate with petals, leaves, feathers. Pierced, Eudora could see, multiple times in the visible ear, possibly also her face or breasts or belly, pressed into the sand, or under her seaweed hair.

Eudora tried to stay present with the woman, what was left of the woman, but lost track of her now and then, first in a thought—maybe she wasn't a woman, but a man, or someone in transition, or one who refused to be defined by anything whatsoever male or female or in between. She had found a person on the beach, a human being. That much she knew—and with all this thinking lost the body, the person herself, himself, themself, whatever of the person was left.

What had led her to assume this body was, had been, a woman, maybe even a girl? The round bottom in tight black jeans, the narrow waist, the delicate wrists, the bare arms—covered in birds and flowers, red and green and blue—the splayed hair.

She wanted to turn her over, but resisted, allowed the curiosity to pass, to fill instead with the presence of loss, of violence and grief.

Why did she assume violence?

Again her thinking took her away. Spinning. To her garden, the lessons of summer. When you give a young tomato plant plenty of room, it grows itself. When you confine it, contain it, it grows tomatoes. How the cultivation of *Solanum lycopersicum* for its fruit exactly paralleled the socialization of women, throughout history and in each single life. She had done both, of course, grown herself and fruited, producing just the one, her daughter.

The thought of her daughter woke her up, brought her back to the beach, the body beside her. The bare tattooed arms, slightly rounded, looking more soft than sinewed. The hands, too, slack in the sand. The fingernails, painted black and silver. She could have been Eudora's daughter's age. A girl. A young woman.

Everything collapses, Eudora thought. Rots and sinks.

Another garden lesson.

SHE HEARD THE police and EMTs before she saw them and stood up from the sand to wave, anxious now, as if she herself had done something wrong.

She looked down again at the body.

"I'm sorry," she said. Out loud. To the girl. To the wind and the seagulls.

For the first time she realized the girl must have been cold, walking on the beach with those bare arms. If she had been walking. If her arms had been bare. Earlier this morning or last night, yesterday afternoon—the days and night had been cold. The sunset had been brilliant, red, orange, pink, indigo, even sometimes black. Eudora had watched it, sitting barefoot on the front steps, wearing a sweater, wrapped in a blanket.

She waved again at the approaching officers, a man and a woman. She noticed how fit they seemed. She saw that the man was Black and the woman Asian, maybe Vietnamese. She had what seemed a cool, almost stony, but beautiful face, and a sadness about her, as if she had seen too many of these anonymous bodies, dead women.

The man did the talking, gentle and warm. His voice invited trust, as did his eyes, so opaque and dark a brown. The longer Eudora spoke with him, answering his questions, the more deeply in her flesh she felt his presence, her response to the heat of him and the weight. He was a fire in the sand.

Meanwhile the woman checked out the cold corpse.

The EMTs had gone. The medical examiner was arriving.

THEY WERE YOUNGER than she was, all of them, the two police officers, the crime scene people, the dead girl, visible now.

"Probable overdose," she heard the Vietnamese officer say, maybe on a phone.

The dead woman might have been pretty once, too, Eudora thought. It was hard to say. Her face was bruised and scarred. She wore a silver nose ring and a stud in her lip. She was not, after all, young. Even dead, her face looked tired, as if she had been tired for a long time. Bring it on, Eudora imagined her saying, before they zipped her into a bag.

She asked the gentle officer if she could go. She told him it was her birthday. "You might have noticed," she added. She had given him her driver's license so he could record her information.

He gave her a smile for that. A little bit of himself, maybe.

"We'll be in touch if we need you," he said, and returned her license.

"Yes," she said. "Of course."

She turned to walk away, uncertain whether to go back to her car or to take the other direction, go on down the beach, continue her walk, her celebration. It didn't seem fair to celebrate now, her birth, her life, and her escape from the life that could have ended like this woman's, overdosed, anonymous, half-dressed, half-buried in sand.

She had been naked on a beach, not this beach, not that long ago. Drunk and naked and having sex with a man she hardly knew. More than a girl then, too. The sun hot, the sand hot. Naked under his naked weight. Not quite naked, not entirely. But naked enough. And drunk. On alcohol but also on the sun and the heat and the flesh, her own and his, the scent of coconut oil and lavender soap and the grains of sand that clung to her skin. Drunk on his near anonymity, on his strangeness to her, his opacity and otherness. Drunk on his desire.

She had said yes to him. Her whole self—body, mind, whatever there was—all said yes. Yes to brunch, yes to tequila, yes to the beach, yes to lying naked in the sand, yes to his hands, to his eyes, his mouth, his teeth, his tongue, yes to his body pinning her, yes to his heart pumping, his heat surging in. Yes to the life of him and the life of herself. Despite the cigarettes, despite the alcohol, despite the devastation. Yes to the onrush of life.

She didn't know that man anymore. Had never, really, known him, and not at all for long. Hardly longer than that afternoon on the beach.

They had not been alone. She had not cared. Other couples were there, some just sunning themselves or swimming, some as naked as she was, some clothed, some eating and drinking and laughing, others having sex. A few people even stopped to watch them. As if they were a movie. And maybe they were a movie. Maybe someone turned on a phone.

Those were the dark days. But now she allowed herself to forget the darkness. She had been alive, and she got out alive, unlike the pierced tattooed woman cold in the sand.

For a moment she wondered whether, after all, she was not alive now, anymore.

No, she didn't wonder. The thought crossed her mind, flew quickly into her notice, that was all, like a little beach bird, off to the side of her consciousness. Not really there.

But then the thought grew louder.

"No!" she said, resisting, and glanced back up the beach to confirm that she was far enough from the police activity that none of them had heard her.

She felt like a suspect.

She wondered whether she would speak with the same handsome officer again, with his caressing near-black eyes. She wondered if she spoke with him whether she would slip up, say something she shouldn't, incriminate herself in some unknowable way, even though her life now was so cleansed of all that had sullied it before.

It was probably not safe to be walking alone on the beach.

The woman was dead. Dead when Eudora found her. Probable overdose. What more was there to say?

"I FELT GUILTY," she said that evening, in a meeting. "As if I should have been the one to die. As if I had somehow killed her."

All around her people nodded.

"It was too weird," she went on. "It's my birthday and there was this dead woman. It really seemed to mean something. But then I realized that was just crazy thinking. There was no real connection."

The nodding died down. She felt the others wanting her to wrap it up, to offer some familiar slogan — *there are no coincidences, stinking thinking, there but for the grace of God* —

"Whatever," she said, and stopped. She looked at all their clean and sober faces. Like her, they were alive. Like her, they all had lived in a misery they now knew they were free of, if only for this day. Even those still struggling, still fighting against recovery, still waking up to pain they had been numb to, knew they had a chance now — by sitting to-gether in this room, got a chance to live. So why did she doubt herself suddenly, herself and them, the whole project of sobriety, just because she had found a woman dead on a beach?

She tried to say this, wanted to say something about it, in a kind of panic, as if her life too had ended, but couldn't find the words to say what she wanted to say. She was afraid of what might come back at her — a compassionate invocation of the dead and the bullet they all so far had dodged, a passive-aggressive attack hidden in plausible deniability, words of encouragement and clubby proverbs smothering what core of wisdom she could not arrive at on her own.

She felt the bitterness in her fear and stammered and gave up trying to express herself.

"I'm sorry," she said. "That's all I have."

She sat stone-faced through the rest of the meeting and left quickly when it ended.

At home she called her sponsor and tried again to say what she was thinking, feeling. After the call she remained dissatisfied. Everything was elusive. As if she had stepped into a great black cave where she could hear only distant voices, dulled, muted, carried in and out on waves. As if she lay alone there, in a damp, chilly darkness. As deeply alone as she had ever been. She tried to breathe in rhythm with the whispers.

From the other side of the duplex, a round of shouting started up, her neighbor and whatever man was with her. Sometimes when she was alone, the neighbor yelled for hours into the telephone. When her little boy was with her, she yelled at him. Sometimes Eudora thought the yelling was just the woman's ordinary level of speech—yelling and laughing and cigarette smoke seeping through their common wall for hours on end. It was hard to tell whether the shouting with whatever man was a danger, to the neighbor or her little boy, whether the neighbor herself might be a victim. The constant volume seemed to be a way of life. Eudora never heard blows or anything breaking, but she always paused, wondering whether to interfere, even to ask for silence so that she could sleep, and always decided against it, in case a request should lead to violence, against herself or the neighbor or both.

In her cave, she made an effort to melt her anger, her powerlessness, knowing that she had been as loud and dramatic not that long before. She buried her head under her second pillow, mentally repeating the words of a song, over and over, or a poem or a prayer, to shut out thinking and resistance to the noise. She had work in the morning. She had her own life. And what could she do anyway? Call the police?

Once in her life, when she was very young, she had called the police. She had lived in another neighborhood then, in a tiny stucco bungalow, her daughter just a toddler, gone for the weekend to her father, when a man came in and sat at her feet, at the foot of her bed, spoke with her back and forth a few times, until she woke to the realization that she wasn't dreaming and screamed. The man ran. She hadn't known what to do next. She had called the friends she thought most likely to be awake that late in the night, in the early morning, the friends least likely of all her friends to think calling the police would be a good idea, and even they said to call the police. She flushed what drugs she had on hand and picked up the phone. A big pudgy white policeman finally arrived and took her statement, looking at her the whole time, she thought, with contempt. She had been drunk before she went to bed. The stranger had walked right in from the driveway through her unlocked kitchen door. The policeman told her to keep her doors locked, to lock her windows, there was nothing more he could do.

Her windows had no locks, so after the policeman left and before she went back to bed, she had hammered nails into the frames to stop the windows from opening more than a couple of inches and the next day called her landlord but got no help.

Her neighbor now, in the duplex, years later, was young, younger than Eudora, and pale and tattooed, like the woman on the beach. She drank beer, mostly, Eudora knew from the bottles and cans she'd seen her carry out. Her name was Jay or Kay or Lacey, something like that, a name that blurred in Eudora's mind with other, similar names. The little boy's name, though, she remembered was Adam. He wasn't always there with his mother, and now and then when they were saying goodbye, she heard her neighbor say, gently and with regret, "I love you, buddy," as if she wouldn't see him again for another long time, or didn't know how long it would be, and Adam would say it back, as if he meant it, "I love you, Mom."

Eudora often doubted that she knew, herself, really, what love was. Still, she could hear something real in their voices.

In the voices the night of her birthday all she heard was rage.

The next day at work she found her hands shaking.

"Not enough sleep," she told her work friend.

"Big celebration?"

She didn't want to talk about it.

ON THE WEEKENDS, after taking care of the garden, she worked in her studio, sometimes painting, sometimes making jewelry. Her studio: the second bedroom that once had been her daughter's, emptied now to make room for a big table and canvas and paper and paint. She sold her jewelry on Etsy, sometimes had a good run after months of nothing. She couldn't read the market but made what pleased her, and now and then someone else would be pleased, and now and then someone else who was pleased would turn out to be a minor influencer and ten or twenty other people would suddenly buy from her. She saved the jewelry money in a special account, from which she bought more jewelry supplies, along with paper and canvas and paint.

She had to open all the windows to work in the bedroom. She no longer lived in a tiny street-level bungalow, but because she had found the woman on the beach, opening the studio windows to circulate air brought that frightened night again to mind. The intruder had run as soon as she screamed. But the policeman had lingered, condescending, treating her like a stupid girl.

The police on the beach had been kinder. The woman had died of an overdose. There was no symmetry between these events. They were linked only by herself, and she herself was not the woman she once had been.

She tried not thinking about these things while she painted, thought instead of texture, color, balance, space, object, image, light—thought not-thinking. But the woman kept coming into view—her hair, her hands, a red and blue and green tattoo.

A FEW WEEKS later, on a Saturday, she was walking into Farmers Market when she ran straight into the Vietnamese police officer from the beach.

"Wow," Eudora said. Coincidence spoke to her, disturbed her. There was that AA slogan.

The woman smiled, warmly, instead of just walking on. She was wearing pale summer clothes and sandals, her black hair loose and long. They were blocking foot traffic in the narrow passageway and moved together into the open. Eudora had only a moment to wonder how she had recognized the officer without her uniform before the woman asked, "Do I know you?"

"I found a dead woman on the beach," Eudora said. "Probable overdose."

"Yes, of course," the policewoman said. "Well that's done." Her name was Agnes. "You're—?"

"Eudora."

"Yes, I remember. Of course. An unusual name."

"Yours, too."

"It was French," Agnes said. "Pronounced in the French way. My French grandfather's mother's name. Family tradition. Like everything else it got anglicized."

"And you're a policeman," Eudora said, not knowing what else to say.

"Why not?" said Agnes. "Another family tradition."

"Why did she die?" Eudora asked. "That woman?"

Agnes shook her head. "Why do they kill themselves?"

When she shook her head, her hair shifted and revealed an earring that Eudora recognized as one she had made. Involuntarily she raised a hand to her own ear. "That's my earring," she said. Her earrings were unique: each individually painted, a miniature canvas, a tiny sculpture made of resin, stone, metal, wood.

Agnes laughed. "No wonder I knew your name. Not *your* name. But the name itself. It means 'good gift.'"

Eudora could not recall how long ago she had made or sold that pair of earrings, or whether she had sent them to someone named Agnes who may or may not have had a French or a Vietnamese last name. She wasn't ready to trust Agnes. She didn't know why. Maybe because she was police. Or because she seemed to want something from her.

"*Agnes* means holy, or pure," Agnes said. She laughed again. "Saint Agnes was a martyred virgin. Also known as Inez or Ines."

After that they wandered in the market awhile, Eudora wondering what they were doing together, too curious to make her escape. She had a shopping list and shopping bags, but really, she had no plans, not even a cat waiting at home to be fed. She should get herself a cat, she thought.

Later that night she looked through her records but could not find Agnes in them.

SHE OFTEN FEARED someone, anyone, wanting something from her. She thought it was probably one of the fears she had drunk to escape. Drinking, she had been fearless. All her adult life, until just a few years ago. But not as a child. And not now.

On Sunday she called her sponsor to tell her about Agnes, not knowing really what there was to tell, but expressing her fearfulness, her paranoia. Yes, she admitted it was paranoia. She tried to take her sponsor's advice, tried to speak up at a meeting, tried to pray. Nothing worked. But she was home and she was sober. Next door her neighbor was playing with the little boy.

Eudora wanted to call her daughter but wanted more to wait until she was at ease. Her daughter could always tell if she'd gone off somehow, spun into some darkness, some fear. She had not even told her yet about the body on the beach, the dead woman, the encounter with the police. How then bring up Agnes, the coincidence of meeting her, as if accidentally, and Agnes wearing those muted blue-and-purple earrings that Eudora herself had made?

She tried work on a new set of earrings. She tried a new painting on paper. Nothing held her attention. She kept feeling the *as if* of the accident of meeting Agnes, the *as if* of finding the body. What was the universe trying to tell her? Agnes had asked for her telephone number. Eudora had wanted to say no but had not known how. Her phone number given to Agnes had felt like an open door, an unlocked window, and still did, because Agnes had not called.

ON MONDAY, COMING in from work, she found her neighbor sitting on the front steps, smoking, weeping. Jaycee or Lacey or whatever her name was moved aside for her to pass as she fumbled with her keys, then called to her from behind—"Wait?"

Eudora turned.

"Can you help me?"

"How?" Eudora asked.

The woman sobbed, hid in her hair, jerked her head up and drew on her cigarette.

"I don't know," she said. "I just think you can."

Eudora waited.

Her original neighbors in the duplex had been a young couple who grew tomatoes in the backyard and had a friendly dog and a temperamental cat and every season swept the jacaranda blossoms from the sidewalk after they fell, not right away, but before they began to rot and slime. Thanks to them, what once had been front lawn was now all English ivy. For years Eudora had been embarrassed whenever they met at the garbage bins or on the steps.

Now her neighbor said, "I hear you sometimes, talking on the phone maybe? You sound so calm. Like you know how to say things to people so they'll understand."

"Tell me your name again?" Eudora said. She should have realized that if she could hear her neighbor, her neighbor could also hear her. She had thought she was so much quieter now.

"Laney," her neighbor said. "I never hear any yelling."

"There's nobody here but me."

"That's what I mean," Laney said. "And you seem happy. When I see you, coming and going, from work I guess. Out in the back, growing your tomatoes or whatever. You don't have any children?"

"A daughter in college," Eudora said.

"See," Laney said. "Adam—" She sobbed and took a long drag on her cigarette and sighed the smoke out. "I think there's no hope for me."

A string of platitudes from three years of meetings ran through Eudora's mind, but not one of them seemed right for speaking. Instead, "I found a body," she said. "On the beach a few weeks ago. A woman. A probable overdose. She had tattoos like you."

Laney nodded, as if this revelation made sense.

"You want to come up for tea or something? For coffee?" Eudora asked.

When she was first getting sober, the old neighbors had shared their garden with her, showed her how they tended their tomatoes, their zucchini, their lettuce and kale, and gave her a bed to plant as her own. In the early mornings they took turns watering from the rain barrel, and when the neighbors moved away to have their baby, the whole garden became Eudora's, the rain barrel too.

"No," Laney said. "Thanks, though. Sometimes I hear you cooking."

"I drop lids," Eudora said.

"Yeah," Laney said, "you do." She laughed. "It always smells good."

"Take care, then," Eudora said.

"Yes," Laney said. "I will. Maybe I will."

ON TUESDAY DURING her lunch break Eudora walked the few blocks to a church where she sometimes went to sit in solitude and silence. Other people also sometimes sat there in the cool darkness, spaced well apart from one another, and sometimes a caretaker or volunteer swept the red tiled floor. Eudora didn't consider herself a believer, but in the empty space itself felt a presence of the sacred, undefined. It was a classic church, made of dark wood and stone and stained glass, and the light changed depending on the seasons and the brightness of the sun.

That Tuesday, sitting alone, she watched the light and shadows play across the dark lifelike figure dying on the cross. A single man abstracted to all suffering human being. Young, old, woman, child, the color of wood, the color of tile, the color of marble, the color of sand. Light and shadow flickered across the body's surface that was not skin, and painted there, in fleeting reds, greens, blues, golds, the dead woman's tattoos.

On Wednesday after work Eudora went to a meeting and out for coffee with her friend, the man she had slept with once and never again. She told him about the dead woman, about Agnes, about the tattooed Christ. He told her about his efforts to get back into school, how hard it still was to believe in himself, sometimes even to care.

"She isn't going to call me, is she?" Eudora said.

"Do you want her to?"

"I don't know. I don't like her hanging out there, unresolved."

On Thursday the jacarandas started dropping their blooms. After work Eudora drove to the beach. She parked where she had parked the day she found the body. She sat in her car and asked herself what she was doing. A criminal, returning to the scene of the crime. She left the car and walked onto the beach by the path she had taken before. She saw no barriers or strips of yellow tape. Just a few planks of broken walkway, patches of beach grass, endless sand. No sign anymore that a body had ever lain here, dead. Or a living being died. Up the beach along the water a man was running with a big black shaggy dog. In the other direction a couple sat side by side at the water's edge. Waiting for sunset maybe. Eudora too could wait for sunset. She was hungry for dinner, but her hunger could wait. She would sit in the sand, in the place where the body had been, where the tattooed woman had died, fled.

She sat there till darkness was almost complete. The sunset had been unspectacular. The man with the dog had come by on the way to leaving the beach and greeted her, polite and distant. The couple had vanished.

By Friday the sidewalk was a carpet of purple. That night Eudora called her daughter.

On Saturday she opened her studio windows and painted, not thinking, just moving in and out of color, texture, light, shadow, shape.

On Sunday she took the broom out to the street and started sweeping. Her old neighbors had left her this task along with the garden. They had taught her instead of clogging the gutter along the curb to gather the swept-up blossoms and add them to the compost bin. She was bathed in purple, from above, from below. The light was brilliant.

While she was sweeping, Laney came out and sat on the steps, watching her, smoking, drinking a beer. "Hey," she said, and waved, her arms bare, exposing the birds and flowers inked there, soaking up the sun.

"Hey," Eudora said. She paused in her sweeping and looked up, overhead, at the purple blooming jacaranda, at the lapis lazuli sky. She would do this day after day, for weeks on end. Even as she swept, new blossoms were falling.

A Vampire Story?

THEY WERE MINOR stars. They met on the set of a series that was shooting in a castle near Prague. They should have been famous. The series was brilliant and maintained a following, especially once it dropped on Netflix. But their timing was bad, or luck, or the choices they made.

Now they lived together and did odd jobs to make ends meet. Sometimes she got a commercial. He accepted an almost invisible role in a single episode of something or other for network TV and died in the opening scene. She barely saw his face, even when they brought him back later as a body on a slab in the morgue. When they weren't acting, they temped, incognito, or waited tables, or cooked or served with a catering crew, careful that the restaurant or gig wasn't one likely to draw people from the industry. They still collected residuals. They still had agents. But they had effectively disappeared.

They were young enough that they could have made another life, but tenaciously held on, to their hopes and ambitions, to their sense of their own beauty, to their love for one another. When they were desperate they sat together in bed watching their still only somewhat younger selves fall in and out of love, and in again. In the series they had played a brother and sister, driven by sensual passion and abhorrence of incest—vampires, metaphoric, not literal. They had played their scenes against the real desire they felt for one another and resisted throughout the three seasons of intermittent shooting, all the way to the finale, when he did or didn't die but either way irrevocably left her.

She had always let herself believe that his character lived, her only evidence the closing shot of the series and his presence beside her in the bed.

At last, at the end of shooting, they had surrendered to the thirst and mystery of their bodies. On set, they had been naked together on several occasions, enacting scenes of unrealizable fantasy, but now their bodies were their own, no longer images, not for sale, and they were free. Still, the traces of their several years of fictional life hung around them, like a gauze, she thought, a silk. A spider's web, he said. Or your hair. They played their parts in bed together, uneasily, unhappily, until slowly, in their bodies, they found themselves again and their fictional selves began at last to fade.

They did no work during that time, despite the concerns and pleas and warnings of their agents.

"I HAVE A history of stopping short," Will said.

"You're too young to have a history," Ursula said.

"No, really," he said. "In my senior year of high school I signed up to do an independent project in place of taking three core classes and instead of doing the work I spent all my time with a girlfriend until the last week when I churned out a barely passing paper. When my dad was teaching me to drive, the first corner I turned I blew out a tire and never drove again."

"How can you live in L.A. and not drive?"

"Uber, Lyft," he said. They hadn't yet returned to the city, not together.

"I rejected the first role they offered me," he said. "I was still a kid. My parents let me say no."

"Lucky for me," she said.

"Maybe not. We'd be sitting pretty. As my dad used to say."

"Like, *When our ship comes in?*"

"That, too."

"Our dads were sort of the same, then."

"Don't go there," he said. He let the implication sink in before he continued. "I pull out of things before they're done."

"Not with me, you don't," she said, as if a sexual joke could disarm his worry. Fail, she thought. "And don't even think *Not yet*. History isn't destiny."

In Los Angeles, living together, sort of, in the apartment she kept with another aspiring and often absent actor, alone together one night as they ate Thai food in bed and watched themselves perform their Renaissance love story with the volume set on mute, she said, mid-episode, "They warned my sister not to marry the man with the bright red car, the steel-toed boots, the little goatee. They told her to give it up, to let him go. But she wouldn't listen. She packed her bags and ran off with him. She's the happiest person I know."

"Like you and me," he said.

She shrugged and turned the sound up as a scene they had shot together began. When it was over they made love, slow and silent, as if her absent housemate was awake in the next room, or as their fictional selves, caught in a nightmare.

"To not make a sound is absurd," he said afterward. "Sound is what we are. Breath is sound. Blood is sound. Muscle and bone and skin and pain and pleasure. Or maybe the problem is in the making, the not—"

"Hush," she said and put two fingers to his lips.

ON A WEIRDLY wet hot afternoon they walked on the beach, sand fleas popping on and off and up and down her naked legs. "I remember a house full of fleas when I was a child," she said. "A tattered couch, faded, rough, teal. I was ashamed of the fleas and the tattered couch. I remember the cats we had then and how they loved us. I remember the sound of my father whistling."

"I think we're done," he said. "I think we need to move on."

"Move on," she repeated. People were walking or sunbathing all around them, but not so many as there would have been if the air had been cooler or dryer or the beach free of fleas.

"The agents are right," he said.

"Really?" she said. "Last night we were getting married."

"That's never going to happen," he said.

When she didn't respond, he walked away and into the waves, cutting through the salty water until she couldn't see his legs and at last he turned to face her. "Come on," he called, "wash away the fleas," and when she reached him he pulled her hard against his body and groped her under the water, fingers sliding between the binding of her bathing suit and her skin and finding her, pushing deeper in. He bit her lip and turned her and pressed against her from behind and kissed her neck and ear and probed until he was fucking her, water splashing with and around them, rolling in and rolling out, hiding and revealing, until, satiated, they collapsed to the soaking sand and let themselves be washed over, held their breaths and surrendered to being swept in from the deep and back to land.

SHE HAD NOT believed him when he said it was over, but that act of sudden sex on the beach turned out to be their last, at least for a time. "Someone is asking a question no one can answer," he said as she drove home. "Every groping for an answer is another question, every answer a refusal. When? What? Why? Why not?"

In the morning he packed a bag.

He was going on a shoot, a freebie, supporting some indie director, starring in her short, a showcase for festivals and grant applications.

For a moment Ursula was jealous of this woman. "No, no," he said, and she believed him. He was always doing shorts and student films and artists' experiments for which he never got paid. What difference did it make? They were who they were, she thought. They would always be who they were for each other.

He was gone for five days, as expected, then for another five.

In his absence she found time to see her agent. She allowed her agent to awaken, if only briefly, her interest in taking another series role. She sat for fresh headshots and saw in them a new and beautiful sadness.

When Will came home he packed everything that was his and moved half a mile away, back to the room he kept in another apartment with other mostly absent actors.

Occasionally they still served together at parties — for what was left of the aerospace industry, or transportation, finance, bioscience, gas and oil, steering clear of music, arts, entertainment, politics. Even so, they were too often almost recognized, despite her simpler makeup and hair, despite his clean-shaven face and the absence of his best-known character's long black curls. It never happened when she worked without him or to him when he worked without her, only when they stood and moved together through one of these busy rooms where they were meant to be invisible as furniture, merely functional in their black-and-white or sometimes red uniforms, offering trays. Instead, in a room together they rearranged space. A pulse, an urgency, palpable, as if in a show of magic, revealed them in all their glamour as their fabulated selves. Inevitably someone saw — often a loner, an introvert, a man or woman standing off to the side of the loudly or softly chattering crowd, scanning, watching. Ursula could see the change in such a person's attention and would find an escape before the seeing became a certainty. But now and then she failed, missed the person or the sign. One night a banker slipped her his card. He wanted them to perform for him, privately. He wanted to watch. At a wedding reception under spotlit palm trees, a woman stared at her and then at Will and back at her, and hours later, after their cleanup, they found the woman drunk in the road, waiting to follow them home. At a corporate headquarters high above the city lights, a man in Buddy Holly glasses backed her up against a wall and said, "I know who you are." She denied it. "What are you doing working this party?" She continued to deny it, inching away from him without success, obstructed by a big potted banana plant, until all at once Will was there, yanking Buddy Holly by the shoulder, away from her, a fist in his face. The plant crashed along with the man. Broken glass, champagne and flutes, shocked guests, a retreat to the kitchen, a caterer torn between laughter and rage, too high to care. They forfeited their pay for the night and found a new service to temp for.

"We should try to not work together," Ursula said on the street.

"I don't know," Will said. "I thought that was kind of fun."

She drove him home and dropped him off, without an agreement or even a kiss.

Usually when he left her, even now, he gave her something to take away—a word, a sensation, an image to tease herself with, a touch, a hint, an allusion. That night there was nothing.

The next time she saw him, he was married.

SHE GOT SERIOUS about finding another role and took every word of advice her agent gave. She sat for another round of photos, going for a harder edge, to balance the wistfulness of the previous set. She enrolled again in acting classes, designed for professionals only. Will continued accepting small parts in quirky little indie projects, comedies mostly, in which he never presented himself as the man she knew he was. As if he had lived a lifetime's worth of ambition and darkness as her haunted brother and was now as done with that complex, driven character as he was done with her. As if he could escape them both just by taking off his spectacular wig.

They had let him keep the wig. Multiple wigs, actually. Mementos of the show.

Someday, maybe, they would be worth a fortune. But only if he allowed himself to become a star.

And his wife, the woman he'd married, wasn't even in the business. She taught third grade. He'd met her visiting her classroom to do a puppet play for the kids.

He lived across town with her now and Ursula rarely saw him. She threw herself into the search for real work, and after accepting a part in the ensemble cast of a Netflix series developed from an old line of comic books, she spent hours every day with a trainer when she wasn't up in Canada shooting. Her makeup was garish and no matter how broad and bad she played, she was told to play broader and badder, an instruction she found both liberating and annoying, but the money and exposure were better than she had seen in years, and once the series dropped, when Will came by to congratulate her, he stayed to binge the first season, eating Thai food with her side by side in bed, for old times' sake, he said.

Before he left, he told her he was leaving his wife. He had not been unfaithful to her or she to him. But he was bored. With everything, he said. It wasn't his wife's fault, but he was a weight on her, bringing her down. To marry her had been a mistake. His mistake. As if he could evade his fate. He had gone back to school. He was studying philosophy and history, he said, when he wasn't volunteering on somebody or other's student film.

IN HIS ABSENCE, Ursula had been careful to avoid relationships. She had had sex with a few men, hookups from the catering world, strangers from one of those random gigs, one-time encounters half anonymous, never with anyone who knew her or ever could know who she really was, never leaving an electronic trail. She did not permit herself surrender beyond the physical, and now that she had a public face again, her options for one-off sex were even more limited. She no longer shared an apartment but rented a small house on a hillside and filled it with plants and a pair of cats and hired a sitter to live in it whenever she was away. Will haunted her fantasies, where she dwelled in her imaginary of him, lover and brother from a simpler and more beautiful world. His breakup with his wife hadn't brought him any closer, and Ursula was often away in Vancouver, shooting the second season, which was longer than the first. As her character's arc gained complexity, she was allowed at last, for a while, to wipe the clownish blood-red lips off her face, but months later, when Will showed up with takeout to binge the drop with her, calling it a new tradition and wearing black silk and denim, his hair long, darker than its natural color and thickened, "Are you in costume?" were the first words out of her mouth.

"You sound like her," he said.

She knew who he meant. "I *am* her. Her voice is my voice."

He started talking at her, in convoluted academic language, about power and menace, parody and kitsch, comparing comic-book characters, comic-book colors and costumes, comic-book plots, with plots and characters drawn from historical records, costumes and colors nuanced and modeled on centuries of European art.

She laughed at him with her comic-book character's stiletto laugh. "Are you trying to grow your wig? Do you intend to be my brother forever?"

They almost fought but backed off, settled down into her pillows and muted their phones to watch, uninterrupted, all fourteen hours of her show's second season. After her character's foray into vulnerability, by the finale she was painted red again—her mask, though a little more lifelike, as impenetrably enameled as before. When it ended they fell asleep together with the cats at their feet and when they woke up the next afternoon they almost made love.

THE WILL WAKING beside her, faux-black hair tousled, with Thai food on his breath, was a lazy imitation of the dangerous, driven lover of her deep desire and devotion. A caricature. He smiled as if a smile was all he needed to win her back, or over. Where was the suffering? The ambition? Buried under layers of kind gesture and graduate-student mannerism? He had wanted to conquer the world. Or at least their world.

"I never meant to be a star," he said, trying to explain himself. "That was you, Ursula. That was all you."

But she didn't believe him. He had been brilliant in the part of her brother.

"The writers made him," Will said. "The period, the history. The wigs. He wasn't me."

"You weren't unhappy then," she said. "All that time. You weren't drifting the way you are now. Do you still have an agent?"

He shrugged and tried to change the subject, to get her out of bed, to feed the cats, to shower, to dress, to go out somewhere for dinner.

"I don't want to go out. Everyone knows me out there again."

"Don't kid yourself," he said. "Nobody knows you. Not even your name. They only know that ridiculous character."

His cruelty confused her. "And what about you? What do they know about you?"

"Me?" he laughed. "My pretty face?"

She asked why he was dyeing his hair. He was reluctant but finally answered. "Part maybe. Superhero movie. Ensemble."

She waited for more, but "Jinx," he said, shaking his head.

"I don't know you," she said. "I don't know you at all."

"Did you ever?"

WHEN THE WIND slammed in from the east, the endless overdry heat intensified their longing for adventure, for change, for sex. They drove, mostly. She drove. Into the hills or up the coast or down to the beach.

Drove in circles, drove wherever speed allowed her, and day after day he rode beside her. They avoided the city and all its playgrounds. She blew her trainer off. The desert was good. She drove straight into it, the heat and the wind, and the air in the desert was cooler. They thirsted, they didn't know for what. Not for each other. They went to the movies. They went to a club. They ate. They drank. They danced. They played cards. They gambled. They went to the races. *Off to the races*, her father used to say every day on his way to work. "No one talks like that anymore," she said. They were walking in the park. They called it hiking. They saw a mountain lion. In her yard they saw deer, a coyote, a rabbit, a feral cat. The wind died but the air stayed hot and the sky filled with the smoke and pinks and reds and oranges of wildfires. Birds still liked her trees, out of reach of the cats. A fog rolled in. After Thanksgiving, Will didn't go back to school. When the rains came, the cats flew into the house, still wild, still chasing one another and the mouse they'd lost inside the stove. The rains brought flood and mudslides.

They still had not made love.

"Nothing is simple anymore," she said.

"We live in a desert," he said. "A desert canyon surrounded by desert mountains, a desert basin opening on a desert beach. We wait for the hot wind and when the wind comes we wait for the rain and when the rain comes we pray for it to end. Nothing we know can survive the fires and heat and rising ocean and even though we know this we just go on and on."

They still had not made love, and then they got busy again with work.

By the time he came to watch Season Three with her, he was married to someone new, already divorcing, and the superhero film in which he had played a small but standout supporting role was in postproduction. She had started Season Three as something like a superhero herself, then passed through an incarnation as a ghoul. By the end she didn't know what she was—fallen monster, victim saint. She began to wonder how much longer she could play this character and fantasized advocating for her own death in the season to come.

SHE HAD OTHER friends and she knew he did too, but their worlds of friends were separate from their life together. A life together, she thought. What a strange idea. Their annual comic-book-series binge, their desert drives. She saw his movie without him, more than once. She liked it better at home than on the big screen. She would have seen everything she loved about him in his small performance, but for its exceptional sexlessness. Then he asked her to be his date for the Oscars.

"You know what that would mean?" she said.

"We'd be seen together? Photographed together? Talked about?"

"What? You want that?" The idea troubled her, not because she wouldn't enjoy being on display with him again, an opportunity to play their old desire in public, before cameras, to pretend to be pretending. What bothered her was his interest in it, his willingness—she couldn't find his motive. "Why?" she asked, but his only answer was "Why not?"

"We'd have to check with the agents," she said. She had not told anyone she was seeing him, least of all her agent.

"They'll love it," he said. "We'll play it for the romance."

"They won't love it. They'll be afraid of another disappearance into catering gigs and anonymity."

"Let them," he said and made a horror-film face at her and horror-film hands. "Be afraid," he said. "Be very afraid." He laughed. "Wear that campy lipstick. I'll wear one of the wigs. We can dress in matching outfits. White shirts with plunging necklines and ruffles and flounces, voluminous sleeves. Skinny black leather pants, hooded red cloaks, boots to the knees. I'll stick to you like glue."

"I don't want to play that kind of part with you."

"What then?"

"Real," she said. "Like a drive in the desert. A job to pay the rent. We were serious once."

"You don't know me," he said. "We can get a deal out of this if we play it right."

"A deal," she repeated.

"Together," he said. "We can work together again."

"As what? Sardonic vampires?"

"Sexy sardonic vampires. Rock stars. Royalty of rock and roll. There's a vehicle for this waiting out there for us. We'll summon it by showing ourselves, twinned at the hip and thirsting. We can drive in the desert forever if we work together again."

THE WEIRDNESS OF the world sometimes overwhelmed her. He got his rock-star vampire movie. He got her to play the part. They fucked on screen and off. She didn't know who he was, or herself. He had been the unattainable throughout her short working life. When he married for a third time — the ingenue victim of the vampire rock-and-roll queen — Ursula attended the wedding. She celebrated her thirtieth birthday reading a pile of scripts. Better scripts, scripts without garish lipstick or black leather pants. She missed him the most when the hot winds blew and she drove to the desert alone. Her long-running comic-book character was not killed off, but her agent got the producers to write the part smaller and smaller, limiting the time Ursula had to spend in Canada. Will had joined the series — someone's cameo idea run amok. She continued missing the Will of catering gigs and anonymity. She looked for a script that could evoke those days of hiding out in ordinariness and invisibility, a script that would give them a chance to perform it, to manifest that moment when, touched by the gods or God, their bodies altered space. She wanted that rush when the fire between them blazed and made them visible. She wanted to see it one more time, that instant of transfiguration, captured on film. She wanted to feel it again. In the doing. In the watching. Without the campy trappings. Without the wig or flaming lips. Without the skinny pants or red capes or bustier or black leather boots. Without the fetish-high heels. It would have to be a comedy, she thought. Comedy was the only solution. Just the two of them, alone, ordinary bodies, working a crowd, offering exotic finger foods and flutes of champagne.

Dangerous

1

It can be dangerous to know a thing, a solitary place. To hold one's breath as a way of shouting. The irresistible tendency to crystalize myth, to manufacture harmony and offer it to others, cunningly rat-proofed, stylish and reasonable, to conceal disorder, too much trouble to stand, to rouse a will, a voice, a terminological gathering, various and nocturnal, so much simpler to collapse, hostile and righteous with caring, sweeping, mopping. Things got ugly quickly, the poet said and went on from there to write a brilliant and famous poem. Things got ugly quickly and every day now they get ugly, with now and then a reprieve.

2

The willingness to erase multitudes, the futility of the commons, inextricable, inexhaustible, diminish the capacity for fate, for prophecy and warning—disaster isolate. Moldering books in bookish wastes, cordoned off, preserved, hoard a plague of fragile misjudgments, in rigorous argument and mourning pages deriding challengers and facile converts, their inadequacy, their contours, their stumbles and missteps. Barriers deprived cede ground. Upheavals spur and lag, their prickly switchbacks fracturing, fragmenting in dead-ends. Where do we go from here? she asks, and gets no answer, but stands in rain and wind to listen just the same.

3

No one can do it for us, momentary insight, walk on water. Many Americans may not know their own collaborationist cunning, ambiguity and interpretation, the cult of nothing missing, nothing hidden. What is your reference system? Sequential, logical, overpowered. Paris, midnight. Where do you find yourself? Inexorable dimensions, clever amplitudes, righteous impartialities. A world without high-heeled shoes and ruby lip gloss, right in the heart of the ancient city. The community demanded a meeting so a meeting was held. The cat is healthy. He takes comfort in your laundry basket.

4

Why make things, when the earth gives magnolias, death-cap mushrooms, shield volcanoes, acidified oceans, caribou? Why be a litter wizard when on every street corner you find a spent syringe? Voice from a nightmare, an ecstatic cascade: People should be scared, it says, obsessive in their breathtaking specificity, delighted, disarmed. Meltwater wreaking havoc, disappearing ice, sheets become a lens. Why make things? Do not force my hand, says the man, steely, handsome, innocent. Or not. Ask a few necessary questions. Not a subscriber? Overlooked? Unclassifiable? Learn the skills and tools you need. Start seedlings.

5

My mother sitting on the edge of her bed, as if waiting for a train, asked what she's waiting for, answers, "Death." When I was a child I walked in cold tide pools poking a tiny finger into the mouths of red anemones. I stumble on the word—*anemone*, not *anenome*. An enemy, a fact, the outcome of the notorious election. *The Lord is my shepherd, I shall not want.* A cloud of sweetness surrounds the first cut daffodils. She sits on the edge of her bed. *The Lord is my shepherd*— Hot red chilis, sesame oil, and miso permeate and ferment cubed tofu until it's creamy and soft. *I shall not want.* "For death," she says. Anenome, anemone. *The Lord is my*— as into the chapel silence at the county jail through the PA system a voice screeches violently its mundane request. *I shall not*—

In Absence

Pelican

She walked to the beach and her cell phone rang.

Odd, she thought—her phone rarely rang, she discouraged anyone, everyone, from using it.

The caller was on the east coast, thousands of miles away.

It was a wrong number—or at least an unintentional call—the caller was not a stranger.

—Odd, he said. —I thought I was calling Sheila.

Sheila, she thought—she remembered Sheila.

—Well anyhow, since you're there, I mean here, he said, how have you been?

—How have I been? she said, or thought—how on earth was she supposed to answer that question?—it had been fifteen years since she'd seen him, or more—eighteen? twenty? yes, twenty—and five, at least, since they'd spoken on the phone.

—Are you still beautiful? he asked, the same as last time—she had thought he would be more original.

Five years ago she had answered that she had gained some weight—asking herself, though not him, *was I ever beautiful?*

The ocean, meanwhile, rolled in, rolled out, blue and green and salty and cool, and seagulls swooped and ravens cawed, while out over the water a pelican dove and she thought she saw a seal bobbing under the waves.

Five years ago the question had surprised her and she had come to afterthoughts, asking herself whether if she had been less honest, or more flirtatious—or wasn't it actually more honest—if she had said what she was really thinking, when was I ever beautiful?—would she then have heard from him again?

Now she says, —Are you original anymore? Do I know you at all?

She isn't sure he's still on the line until she hears him say, —Well, I've been fine, pretty good anyhow, thank you for asking, not so depressed anymore, and I'm getting married again.

—Since you're here, she says, there I mean, I wonder, I have to ask, really—well never mind, maybe I don't—but really, she thought, he had been married more often than anyone she knew and was depressed more often than anyone she knew, had tried more various anti-depressants than anyone she knew—but really, really, she thought, there was something altogether *other* at the bottom of him that she would never grasp.

What she said was, —Sheila. I remember Sheila.

—Oh no, he said. —I'm not marrying Sheila. I was just calling her.

He was not a stranger, for all his mystery—she knew this just calling person very well. Thousands of miles away, on another coast, decades of another life, a life entirely beyond her grasp, and yet there was still and always had been this knowing between them. She almost acknowledged it—the strangeness and the knowing, the peculiar luck of his accidental call at a moment when her phone would ring and she would hear it, which it rarely did and she rarely could, to tell her again, as he had so often told her, at one of these many turnings, that he was leaving his wife, or starting with another, or changing his meds, or more depressed, or less.

I was just walking to the beach, she thought about saying—it's the only place my phone works—but paused and breathed and looked out at the water.

—Maybe you'd better call Sheila then, she said, and watching the swooping bird and bobbing seal, said again goodbye.

Water

The water laps pink and silver on the shore after the sun drops below the tree line across the marina. Gliding seagulls catch a gleam of gold.

He had stayed out all night and came home to a silent, empty house. He ignored his sense of panic and went to bed.

—I can't believe you did that. What were you thinking?

Cries. Voices from across the water.

—Well, somebody had to.

Later he woke up and saw the flowers, the lavish, many-colored lilies she brought in from the garden every day.

—That's not the point.

—And the point would be?

The smell of smoke, charcoal, barbecue mingling with the salt air and incense and lavender—

—*You. You.* Why did *you* have to do it?

But she was gone.

He made some coffee, evening already coming on.

—You don't know me at all, do you?

Lilies closing up shop for the night, pink, blush, orange, luminous red in the after-sunset light.

He would go out again and stay out again and be alone in the silent empty house again.

—No. Not really. Evidently I don't.

The water lapping silver still, rings circling out from the myriad tiny moored boats.

One white sail slowly passing.

From now on.

Late Afternoon

The late afternoon sun through the window glass was blinding. Her leg hurt and she was hungry for dinner. Outside a woodpecker hammered at a tree. She didn't know where she was, or who she was, or what she was doing, sitting in cold sunlight, blinded.

Someone came near her, bringing something that almost smelled like food, seemed to be food—her stomach responding.

She seemed to remember this person. She seemed to remember better food.

—What is it? she heard herself ask, but she meant to ask *Who are you?*

—Tomato soup, said the woman—she understood this was a woman.

—And a grilled cheese sandwich, the woman added, the voice somewhere behind her now, above her and far away.

Odd, she thought, and she noticed that the bright sunlight had shifted, and she was colder than ever, and her leg no longer hurt and her hunger was gone and she could no longer smell the sandwich or the soup or hear the voices that she somehow nonetheless sensed were still whirling about her, more of them now, as if that were possible.

Somewhere behind and above and far away there was light again, a different sort of light, almost a rainbow, maybe, and she remembered something, a thing like a grilled cheese sandwich, but it had no taste or texture or body.

—Tomato soup, she said and tasted the words as if they filled her stomach and tasted that she had no stomach.

—Who is it? she said and —What are you? but all she heard was laughter, and music.

She remembered nothing but saw miracles of color and flavor and texture and heat and coolness and knew there were no words for these things, for this, no word for any of it. She remembered nothing but heard a person, felt her, knew her, a woman—a daughter? a mother? a sister?—no word for this woman, no remembering, just the feeling and the knowing.

The woman came near her, nearer, and passed right through her or she passed right through, or there was no through and no place for passing.

She didn't know who she was or where she was or why she was blinded in the cold light.

In time she heard a hammering, as of nails, as of a coffin.

She felt no pain and she was not hungry but knew dinner was coming, a dinner for her and of her and on her, all in her honor and beyond her. The late afternoon sun in the glass blinding, and there was no sun and there was no glass and no late, no afternoon.

Over

She had gone to see her mother who was dying. She didn't know she was dying, she or her mother, they only knew she was sick and old—mostly old.

Eucalyptus grow along the road here, their gray, green, and sometimes red and silver leaves rising, falling, dying in the dust.

—It is not okay.

—Did I say it was okay?

They are ancient trees, and their perfume strong—sharp, bright, pungent, that unique eucalyptus tang.

When her mother arrived to live with her she had seemed older suddenly—much older. A month or two later she fell, a month later, and two months later, and another month after that.

—You're ignoring me again.

—Honey, it's not ignoring you. I'm just busy. You need work of your own.

—You're kidding, right?

A bell rings in the distance, the near distance, rolling slowly up the canyon, a big deep temple bell.

She needed more help, they needed help. She couldn't take care of her mother alone.

The sun has not yet risen, moonlight the only illumination, the gray green red and silver trees all moony-toned and cool.

—Did I say I was kidding?

The first bird trills, sings, then another.

—I think this is over now, I really think this is over.

She started smoking, and then she stopped.

A wind starts to rustle leaves, a wind as if from nowhere, from the dust.

She sat with her mother, and then her mother died.

Rain falls, a drop here, a drop there, a mist more than a rain, cool on the cool skin.

Permission

—I want your permission to tell her what you just told me.

The stove was crackling but the room was cold, flames eating wood, but giving off no heat.

—My permission?

A little boy wearing a rainbow knit cap and a book bag walked with his mother to the beach. On the way he saw a horse and a dog.

—It will help the situation. I think it will help.

Outside, the rain poured down, drumming on the roof, in the trees.

Only the fire and the lightning cast color into the room, first hot, the illusion of hot, then white, or lavender, and cold.

At the beach his mother met a man.

He did not know the man, and stood behind his mother, clinging to her long blue skirt.

A wind rose up, you could hear it, through the trees, a howling and a beating against the glass panes.

—I don't feel so comfortable with that, having you repeat it, speaking for me.

The darkness of the night was absolute, except in the bursts of light.

—You don't trust me?

His mother was very pretty and the man made her cry.

—It's not that.

The boy kicked the man and kicked sand at the man and ran away from his mother and the man and her pretty blue skirt and ran back alone past the dogs and the horses and he knew his mother would chase him and the man might chase him too and when he was sure no one could see him he ducked off the trail into the scrub grass and behind some big rocks and dropped himself down and hid.

Smoke began to pour back into the room, or the smell of smoke, lavender and gold and white.

—You won't stand by your words?

More wood on the fire, all the wood at once, to raise the flames, to bring up the heat, to make it through the night.

On the trail they found the rainbow cap and the red book bag, but his sandwich wasn't in it and the little boy was gone.

In the Heat of the Day

You sit in the heat of the day, the breeze blowing close, light shimmering, flies and flowers dancing in their skin. You want to move, to walk, to run, to join the dance. But you are tired, find yourself again and again in the heat, in the glow, in the density of air and stillness, tired.

The barking dog doesn't quit—where is the action?

You get up from your chair, your chaise lounge in the shade with the bright bouquet on the table and the late afternoon birds sailing on the wind, the four o'clock bell chiming from the church tower.

You get up from your chair. You have someplace to be—where? You turn your gray head to the white butterfly, and another, and another.

From the window we see your confusion, only confusion, your turning head.

—Grandma! the little one says.

Who—you?

The little one, blue and pink and green with orangey hair and big eyes that stare at you calling out that word to you, as if it's your name, more and more excited—we can see, and the little one crying now—why?

You look at us, up here in the window, you blink in confusion and turn away.

White butterflies circle your gray head, your curls in the bright light, become your curls, as if your curls. You look every which way, lost, like a little girl lost, without moving, as if you have somewhere to go, but where? Because you cannot move, you are held in that fixed state of your last hour, your last breath. You would get up if you could, get up from your chair, from what is left of your life, and you would leave us, who seem to you to be on the other side of a window—

And we are.

The church bell chimes the late afternoon hour, the five o'clock birds sailing on the wind, and a cat runs past to pounce—at what?—bird, butterfly, mouse, shrew? The barking dog starts up again, and you are tired in the fading heat and the darkening glow.

You are ready to join the dance.

You are ready to shimmer, to fly in the breeze, to shed your dying skin.

Satiety

Choral song from the church across the street, helicopter overhead, child's cry and laughter—all came through the loft window on the morning breeze.

—He told me to get off the train.

—Why would he do that? I don't understand.

—How should I know? Maybe he was just wrong.

The white and brick plaster walls shimmered and shadowed with sunlight and leaves.

He got up that morning and left the house. He knew he would not be back.

Bacon, pancakes, maple syrup, coffee—strawberries and cream—first a sight, then a smell, then a taste, and the dense heart of satiation.

—Maybe he's a bully is what I think.

The yellow table gleamed.

He didn't know but he knew it was the end of this particular life.

—I don't get you, why would you think that? He's a perfectly nice man.

The stainless steel glistened.

He walked out the door into the bright morning.

—Oh yes. Perfectly nice. Picks a fight with you and throws you off the train.

—Did I say that?

The glass shot diamonds onto the walls.

The clock struck one.

He stepped into the street.

He crossed.

He turned the corner and disappeared.

Agency

HERE IS THE situation: they work together, a man and a woman. Neither is boss of the other and they progress at more or less the same pace. Over time they become friends, and later lovers. Neither feels harassed or abused. Every move they make on the trajectory of their affair is consensual. He desires her. She desires him. Neither is married or otherwise committed. No favors are exchanged. No work advantages or disadvantages are part of the conversation. Nothing work related is at stake. They are friends and respect one another, and later, drawn by desire, when they come together, for a while they love.

Inevitably, things change. They compete for the same promotion. In the tension of uncertainty their sexuality waxes and wanes in unfamiliar ways, retreating, or rising with greater force, an exciting almost dangerous aggression, first from her, then from him, and again from her. Each sees the other, briefly, as a stranger. Desire intensifies, intimacy fades.

She gets the new job, the new title, the private office, the expense account, the raise. She begins to travel. He withdraws from her sexually. His jealousy grows. He flirts with other women at the firm and, after hours, in bars. He calls her less frequently, lets her initiate contact, shows up for her when invited—often brutally, or drunk.

What she means by brutally: no, he isn't violent. But he is cruel, cold and withholding, or vicious with complaint, criticism, contempt, harsh words. She could leave him, but she can't.

He looks for another job, at competing agencies, imagines besting her elsewhere, securing a better title, a bigger office, a higher raise, a more famous client list, an unlimited expense account. These fantasies excite him and prepare him to face her in her bigger bedroom, to satisfy her in her bigger bed.

The more he is with her, the more brutally he treats her—yes, he is willing to own the word—the more her desire seems to demand from him, as if with her new responsibilities she has become insatiable.

He begins to think he should ask her to let him go, but feels bound still to her body, and withdrawing from her—his withdrawal—increases her demands. He likes her demanding body as she likes his brutal body withdrawing.

She too thinks she should ask him to let her go. But where would she find another man to touch her as deeply as this one has, as this one does? She sees men, attractive men, and once almost slept with one, as if to free herself from his hold on her, until at the last minute she retreated, changed her mind.

She thinks a promotion, or a better job at another firm, would help him, would help them both to find their way back to mutuality, to respect, but she knows that to do anything on his behalf would taint his accomplishment, and would compromise her own integrity, and the integrity of their relationship, whatever might be left of it.

He has another explanation for why she won't help him: she knows, or fears, that as an equal and competitor he would not need her anymore, would not crave her, would not come to her bed and her body. He says this to her in the night, when he is fucking her, bruising her, holding her hostage to his will. With his only power filling her, she fears what he says is true, and acknowledges this fear, yielding, surrendering to anything and everything in the surrender of her flesh.

He can find no way out, but collects young colleagues to confide in, younger women—cautiously unlayering his life, revealing only a little, and a little more. He makes his confidences in quiet corners at parties, in bars, or during lunchtime walks in the park. He takes advantage of the younger woman's sympathy until he feels it's safe to breach professional decorum. His language gets more graphic. His hands draw closer to forbidden regions of her flesh. Sometimes he touches her. He always leaves her hanging, wanting more, and takes his brutal arousal back to the woman he would like to leave.

She knows what he's doing and doesn't care, as long as he comes to fill her. He knows she doesn't care and in that moment he doesn't care either.

But both are tiring of this game. It is a game of chicken now: Who flinches first?

What if he abandons her for one of those younger women? Would she accuse him then, of emotional assault or battering or even rape? Would she harass him, come after him, stalk him, continue making demands? Could she contain herself? And if she cuts him off forever? Would he turn on her, charge her with harassment, abuse of power? And the young women? What if they spoke up, against him, or her, or both?

How has it come to this? They were such good friends once, not so long ago. They entered into their relationship with such innocence, with such good hope. Now neither can bear to look at that time, how naïve they were, how feckless.

They walked in the park one day. It was lunchtime. It was spring. They saw blue jays harassing a feral cat. They tried to rescue the cat and the cat scratched her. They went to a drugstore and bought rubbing alcohol and cotton and they sat in the grass and sunshine while he cleaned her scratches, which ran all the way up her bare arm. She kissed him. Or he kissed her. Together they were kissing. They were smiling, laughing, crying. They called in, separately, and didn't go back to work that day. They went to his apartment, which was small, and dark, even on a sunny April afternoon. They were kind to each other, and gentle. She was in love. He said he was. She said she was too.

Claudine

HER FATHER WAS a world famous intellectual and Claudine an unknown dancer. For many years she had lived as far away from him as possible. But now she had come home. During the years when she kept her distance, she would allow him a restaurant meal at times if he was passing through New York. Otherwise, they rarely spoke, and even at those meals mostly he did the talking while she ate whatever bloody meat he was paying for and listened or pretended to. She noticed this only now that she had returned to the city of her birth and childhood and met again the noisy teenager she had been. She had lost that young Claude somewhere along the way. By moving across the country in order to grow up, to become Claudine, she had left herself behind.

"It was a long time ago, of course," her friend said, as if to cross over a moment of awkwardness. How long had it been since they had seen one another? How long since Claudine had come back to this place—this city, this neighborhood, this street, this house that her friend still called home?

Not in lifetimes longer than the years, and even when she had participated in the charade of going home for a holiday or whatever, that concession had not brought her to the neighborhood of her childhood. Her father, too, had moved on, up, even while she still lived with him, had broken through from obscurity in the academic shadows to celebrity and public renown.

It was still his world, her father's. The satisfaction, the destruction—the speed, the darkness, the lights, the days, the nights—the power, would all, always, be his.

"No one ever lived here planning to stay," her friend from childhood said. "The families my mother grew up with were long gone by the time I was born. The families I grew up with all moved away. Just like you. To be third generation in this house is as weird here as falling snow. To live in a house without a mortgage. To drive the car that belonged to my mother. To be unmarried. To have no lover. Not to date. Never to wear high heels or makeup. Not to care. I wouldn't even know this if not for you."

Claudine said, "I can't forgive him."

He had hold of her mind—so many years later he still had hold.

But not of her body. Never again a claim on her body. Not he or any-one would ever desire her body again. Not even dance students, not for what it could teach them, not for the work it could do. No one. She had let all that go. Discipline. Rigor. Violence. Energy. Joy.

"It was so long ago," her friend said again.

Time had changed everything and nothing, Claudine thought. Past and present pressed together, superimposed, inextricable.

"Only the street names are the same," her friend went on.

Flowers to the west: Rose, Begonia, Dahlia, Foxglove; to the east, the names of trees: Hawthorn, Pepper, Palm, Yew—a mélange of the local and the nostalgic.

"Did we notice?" Claudine asked. "On Lilac, we lived side by side between them, Bougainvillea one block over, Jacaranda one behind, and never knew to which world we belonged."

Cheap, spacious houses, with sandy lots and trucked-in lawns. Hot, dry, sunny, sometimes flooded. In drought-free years, the little girls ran through sprinklers all summer long, just as their mothers had done.

But they lived in drought more frequently than their mothers did, in longer lasting droughts, and drier. "We saw fire in the hills," she said.

When her friend's mother was a child, the trees planted one per house in the strip between sidewalk and curb had been stunted little things, but by the time Claudine and her friend were children the little laurels grew leafy and almost tall. Now they made dense shade.

"We laughed over our parents' photographs," Claudine said. Black and white images, tight waists and poofy skirts, permed hairdos, big cars with shark fins.

"Our high school photos look just as strange and antiquated to our daughters now," her friend said.

"I have no daughters," said Claudine.

It was her father's city. It would always be his city.

WHEN SHE WAS eleven, her parents had left what her father later called "that tacky subdivision" for Silver Lake, moved into a house with terra cotta floors and Spanish arches, white walls and heavy dark wood tables, benches, chairs, in the yard a lemon tree, bougainvillea growing up to the red Spanish roof and along the fence, in back a small swimming pool lined in blue-and-white arabesque tile, in front a steep hillside, terraced with pots of cactus and geranium, brick stairs winding up from the street to the porch where the young Claudine sat out at night in the semi-darkness and imagined the stars.

For a while, encouraged by her mother, who wanted her not to develop a superior attitude based on her suddenly elite dance education or the rise in their social status, Claudine had gone back to the old neighborhood for occasional sleepovers, until in time her friend's house became a world of guilty pleasures: dressing up in the brother's black leather, in sexy lingerie they fabricated from silk scarves, in the mother's high-heeled shoes, dancing dirty, together and with their own images in mirrors, thumbing through girly magazines Claudine recognized only later as having been softly pornographic, eating ice cream, pizza, and chocolate, smoking clove cigarettes and marijuana found in the brother's pockets, drinking strange cocktails, juice or soda spiked with a splash of this and a splash of that, skimmed off any bottle they found open whenever they were alone in the house. The brother had gone to the army. His room was a treasure trove.

In her new world Claudine was a good girl. Got good grades, didn't smoke, didn't drink, didn't date. Danced and only danced.

Her father had converted an extra bedroom into a studio and hired young dancers to prepare her for professional training. He liked the young dancers and seduced them when he could. Three times a year, he sent Claudine on month-long intensives with cutting edge companies thrilled with her for being her father's daughter. More and more her mother vanished, until finally she was gone.

In her mother's absence, Claudine ate in secret and puked.

She knew, even then, that she wanted to get away, to go places, to see the world. At the same time, every day, she wanted never to leave the house.

She had carried both desires with her, both impulses, into the future, into loves and losses, successes and failures, travels and sojourns, into big empty lofts and small dark rooms—into what she now understood had been her only life.

WITH HER FRIEND again, after so many decades, Claudine felt herself simultaneously a stranger and deeply known. Anywhere else she would have blushed at the unfolding memories of their dress-up games, their little drunks, their experiments with drugs and makeup, but sitting in the very house, looking at herself and her friend in the very mirror, holding in her hands the same silk scarves, wearing again the brother's old leather jacket (a better fit than when she was a child), drinking even from the same red glass (really? "Really," her friend said), she felt them again, all over, the adventures of curious children, their learning of their world.

And her friend had stayed. Never left. Not even when she got married. Not even for a honeymoon. "Went to a dude ranch in the desert," she said with a shrug.

"That must have been the last time I saw you," Claudine said.

"No. You stopped by once later. When Julie was born."

"The baby," Claudine said. Of course. Funny little thing.

"There were two more after her. Also girls."

All gone now, Claudine thought. As gone as her own life in dance. Far away. Universities. Jobs. North. East. One in Japan. "Grandchildren?" she asked, not because she cared but because she saw that the question might be painful to her friend, as painful as her own unfinished career.

"I try to stay connected. They loved me when they were little. But as they get older, less and less—

"They've all grown beyond me," her friend said after a silence. "Just like you."

Claudine shrank. In the tone she heard why everyone who had ever loved her friend had left her, and knew this tone was her own now too, or threatened to be, nothing surviving but ravenous complaint.

She looked at herself in the mirror, the brother's black biker jacket, vintage now. She zipped and unzipped it, tilting her head, as if seeking an effect. She imagined her little breasts without the shirt underneath, without the tank top, just the jacket and her skin. Her skin of long ago. The big brother's boy smell rubbing up against her virgin flesh.

She knew she was too young to think of her life as over. They both were, but her friend had given up to that way of thinking, a decade or even two before. For Claudine the growing sense of life ending was a mystery. Not to imagine possibilities, no one-door-closes-another-door-opens self-coaching, no stoking the will to continue, to discover and make something new.

If this sense of an approaching end was not entirely a mystery, until now it had always appeared with a companion, a dream of something better, something other, a performance, a place, a person. A way forward more than out.

Now, for the first time, the sense of everything coming to a close arrived uninvited and solitary, unbidden and alone.

So here she was. Back at the beginning. Circling the beginning. Unwilling to go deeper in. Unwilling to call her father. Unwilling to smile at him or at his accounts of his latest projects or at the shelves piled with translations of his many books. Unwilling to embrace his other—newer, younger—daughter or her children or his wife. Unwilling to be Aunt Claude again, even one more time. Unwilling to be his little darling. His failed little darling. Unwilling to go on display among his celebrated friends. Her small triumphs trumpeted, her enormous failures ignored.

Instead she sat nestled into a shabby old couch drinking nostalgic whatever's-in-the-cupboard cocktails, wearing silk scarves and vintage leather, fantasizing her own breasts in the hands of a teenage boy long dead in some desert or jungle, tuning out the lamentations of her former friend.

"I'm a terrible person," she said suddenly, aloud.

Her friend, interrupted, laughed, as if she had simultaneously heard and not. "You're only just finding that out?"

WHEN CLAUDINE LEFT her friend she drove haphazardly, wantonly, still wearing the leather jacket. She was cold, she had said. Underdressed. For old time's sake, she said. It will help me meet my father. In the end she had traded for it—gave her friend the $700 high-heeled Guccis thrown loose into the trunk of the rental car, never yet worn. In her friend's bathroom before she left she had peeled off her shirt and tank, rolled them into her bag, and zipped the leather up to her clavicle, and all the while as she drove she imagined herself unzipping. She imagined her father's face. She imagined a gun in her pocket. She laughed and shook out her hair. All four windows were down. She had no destination. She thought about stopping, getting a room for the night, sleeping it off. She laughed again, louder, turned on the radio, cranked up the volume.

She wanted to drive for speed but the city's arteries were clogged. To reach an open road she would have to go out to the desert or up toward Bakersfield and the 5. The 101 was slower at first but in the end would be a better ride. She would stop in Santa Barbara maybe, or go farther up the coast. Walk around San Simeon. Pay homage to the text that had made her father famous.

In the end she got only as far as Malibu, strolled on the beach, sat in the sand, watched the sun go down, unzipped her naked breasts for the stars.

When she woke the morning light was not yet risen, a few stars or planets still visible in the fading sky. She was cold. She still had the jacket, the car keys in a pocket, her pills, her shoes. She had slept alone on the sand for hours and not a soul had bothered her. Only her father, in her dreams, where she had danced for him, wearing a skirt of swirling silk and the leather jacket, in the body of the adolescent she once had been. Her friend sat by and watched, but her father stood, came closer, grabbed her wrists, one after the other, and held her firm, staring at her nakedness under the scarves and at her breasts until finally at her eyes. At, not into. That stare was all the dream gave her: that and his grip on her wrists, which even now felt bruised.

DRIVING BACK THROUGH the sleeping or early waking city toward what once had been her home, her father's house, she told herself that she knew what she had come for. She might not know when or where, but she did know how. She had that much of a plan. She had once attended a training in first aid for mental health. She had learned from it how to keep her own secret. If she had been hesitant, conflicted enough to reveal her intention to anyone, to her childhood friend, say, according to the training that confidante was supposed to ask her whether she had a plan. If she answered yes she did, the friend should ask whether she had means to execute it, and if she answered yes again, the friend should immediately call the police.

Knowing this, Claudine had said nothing to her friend. Going to see her had been perhaps a test of her own resolve, a practice run. To meet the past and keep silent. Next, she would see her father. Just like this, naked under the leather jacket. Almost the lithe young Claude of her dream.

She had meant to show up wearing the Guccis as weapons: skinny jeans, red tank, see-through oxford shirt, impossible shoes. But the jacket was better. It had history. It smelled of boy, and of time long gone. It would speak loudly her contempt for her father. Or her anger. She wasn't sure what. She turned the volume up on the radio.

She had quarreled with her friend before she left. It was a quarrel that brought their history back to her, her friend as bully, finding fault, always picking a fight that Claudine could never win. She had felt again the anxiety of younger, more malleable times, when she tried to adapt herself to her friend's complaints, each adaptation leading to a new objection, a new confrontation. She had forgotten all this, or set it aside, imagined perhaps that after so many years this way of being together would no longer manifest itself when they met face to face. Still, it had, over nothing—whether to have another drink? whether to smoke or order pizza? whether to sit inside or out?—and with it had come every old quarrel, each unique and always the same, Claudine blamed for something that remained opaque, then for not understanding, for the friend not feeling understood. Claudine also felt not understood, always, but did not think the failure of understanding was exactly her friend's responsibility, did not imagine her friend could somehow become other than whoever she was in order to cough up whatever understanding she might be willfully withholding. Such an impossible transformation was what Claudine felt her friend expected of her, even demanded; but saying this, she knew, would be more trouble than it was worth. As always, her friend expressed frustration that they couldn't talk about their disagreement. Still, Claudine withdrew. She had never been able to express an observation about the dynamic between them without adding to the drama. They used the same words but the meanings always differed. The more they talked, the more she would lose. It was a double bind. Anything she said would be turned against her. As would her silence.

In this, her friend was like her father, Claudine thought. Or saw. Saw suddenly. And again. The two of them—wanting her to be who she wasn't in order to meet their own unspecified needs.

She had always known this and as often as she forgot it was not surprised. She had no energy for sorting it out. What energy she had she would conserve for him.

Then she saw him too, as clear as dreaming. His handsome face, his gray eyes and silver hair.

She drove to recharge.

She was hungry but stopped only once, for gas and a pee and a bottle of water, the sun and its light finally visible.

SHE PARKED A block away from the house and sat in the car listening for a few minutes to the news before getting out and walking along the sidewalk and up the red brick stairs. The porch had new wicker furniture since the last time she had been here, and bright colored plastic toys, for her half-sister's children, she guessed. She had no feeling for those children, or for the sister. They were strangers to her, part of the life her father had made after Claudine's mother left them and after Claudine moved away. Sometimes she wondered about that second family, whether their father was kinder to them than he had been to her, whether he controlled them as he had her, whether he ever had touched them in loving and frightening ways. She knew her father had no memory, no belief in having done even one thing wrong. And maybe he never had. She had asked him about this during one of those meals in New York. "It was all so long ago," he said.

He had been a drunk when she was a child, not a bad drunk, functional, driven by ambition. By the time they met for dinner in New York, his appetites were tamed. Hers were still problematic. After dinners with him, she stuck her fingers down her throat.

"You have to forgive me," he said.

"I don't," she said. "What does my forgiveness matter?"

He had his new wife by then, his new child, halfway grown.

"Tell me you won't go spreading these stories around."

She shrugged. His fame meant nothing to her. His reputation. He could keep them. She told him as much.

"What do you want then?" he asked.

"Nothing," she said. Even then. Nothing.

And that was the truth.

SHE SAT HERSELF down on one of the new wicker chairs. She wondered whether she would ring the doorbell. She thought maybe not. She slipped off her canvas flats and tucked her feet up under herself. She would just sit and wait. She was putting herself in his hands one last time. If he found her, she would be saved. If not, not. A roll of the dice. If she was lucky, she would fall asleep and never wake up. She didn't know whether there would be pain. She had not investigated. She had feared interference. As if some AI might infer from her searches an imminent threat to herself and, less wary and more intuitive than a friend, notify the police.

FOR A LONG time, she had been saving up a stash of pills. She had no idea what they would do to her. She didn't know, really, whether she would even die. There were just so many of them, she thought they would have to accomplish something.

She felt her heart suddenly thrum in a flutter of panic, not because the pills were already doing their work, but at the recognition that if she got nauseated or seized up in a cramp or some violent pain, she might cry out for help, involuntarily, could, all against her will, alert the universe to her body's desire to live.

She had left her phone in the car, and her bag, everything but the rest of the pills and the bottle of water. If she sat too long without effect she would take more. She was sorry now that she had wasted the night on the beach. It would have been good to see the stars one more time from this porch that had been her refuge during those nights when inside, in the house, her father and mother negotiated their terrible end.

Instead the day was bright, already hot.

She unzipped the jacket.

She stood up and stumbled a bit on her way toward the back, to the pool. She would go for a swim, she thought. She felt lightheaded, giddy. She didn't remember why. At the thrill maybe of taking her clothes off outside her father's house. She almost laughed but her mouth was dry. She drank from her bottle. Something was going wrong with her body. She couldn't sense what exactly. Her feet didn't land where she meant them to land. Her eyes didn't see color in the usual way. Her skin was wet and dry at the same time. Her mouth tasted like chocolate. She smelled fire. Music roared in her head. Beethoven. Angels. Messengers of God. The Messengers. Her city. Her father's city.

THE MAILMAN HAD found her, her father said. Half undressed and sprawled on the terraced hillside. "Thank God it wasn't Cassie," he said. Cassie, his younger granddaughter, on her way in from school.

Claudine refused to look at him, to speak to him, although in her mind she could see him anyhow, the thick hair, the pale eyes, the taut lips, and when he was gone she would instruct a nurse not to let him visit again. Hearing his voice was bad enough, thick and liquid and throaty. She could almost feel the spittle as he jabbed the air with one long elegant finger.

He was paying for the hospital, of course—the rehab, halfway house, whatever it was. How else could she lie here recovering at leisure in such a lovely, private room?

Maybe she had made her point.

But she had not intended to make a point. She had failed in this as in everything else. Her accident, they would call it. Her father and his wife and their daughter and the two little girls, the son-in-law already no longer on the scene.

When she first woke up, she had remembered nothing, knew only surprise at the sound and light and color surrounding her, not even the objects they signified. They sorted themselves first into words—white, red, yellow, green, orange, blue, voice, machine, beep, horn—and then, vaguely, into things: walls, doors, flowers, tray, blanket, window, monitor, car. She became aware of her hand, the left, which felt like lead. A clamp restrained the index finger; a tube stuck into the back of the hand was taped to the skin. Above her an IV pouch glittered in angled sunlight, flooding through narrow venetian blinds. Nothing had ever been more beautiful.

She remembered the rental car, the first particular she had wondered about. As best she could, with only her glance, she had searched the room for her clothes, her bag. She had wondered whether she could move. Lifted one leg, then the other. The rhythm of beeps from the monitor beside her intensified. As if she had been dancing, she thought, and gave a little mental laugh. She stayed in the bed. Her clothes must be in a closet—a feeling stirring that had been dormant, maybe for a long time, although she had no sense of time. She wanted to leave the hospital. She wanted to go back to the beach, to walk all night and gather stones. She knew what her mistake had been. It was not her father's fault. With all that she blamed him for, in that moment nothing had ever been his fault. She had wanted to shame him and she had failed. But something else had happened, something better. She had gone beyond him. She had left him behind.

Still, when he came to sit beside her to tell her what had happened, what she had done and almost done and what the story was to be, how she was from then on to live, she refused to speak to him. She didn't need to hear it. She knew him too well and believed what she knew. He could no longer surprise her. But she could surprise herself. The light coming in the window told her so. The yellow of the daffodils, the purple iris, the red and white lily, the orange rose.

Her father had brought or sent these flowers. Her father or his wife or her not-so-little half-sister. Maybe even her one-time friend, although she doubted her friend could know anything about this, where she was now, or how it was turning out.

The flowers, wherever they came from, had more to say to her anyhow than whoever had provided them. They were untouched. They glowed.

Claudine suspected that if she let her father see how happy she was, how suddenly euphoric — or the nurses or the doctors or anyone at all — they would recognize her resolve and obstruct her, so she took care not to show them her heart. She would enact recovering slowly. She would, as if patiently, watch the news and movies streaming into her room. She would eat, pretend to eat. Little by little, she would gain access to her clothes, her shoes, her cards, her phone. She would wait for a spring tide, a full moon. She would slip away in silence, first out of the hospital, then through the streets, toward the coast, across the highway, to the beach. No one would find her, ever again. She would dance, one last time, for the moon and the stars, draping herself in seaweed, on flat wet sand made naked by the outgoing tide. She would fill her pockets. She would walk into the receding waves, until her pockets weighed her down. She would drop to her knees. She would thwart the will of the body to live. She would make angels in the sand, messengers to be erased when she was erased. She would watch the stars until the tide turned and the waves paused and rolled back in. She would not be making a statement for her father. Or a gift. Her life had nothing to do with him anymore. The stars would never miss her, and she would no longer miss or long for the stars. She would lie there until she woke up the hunger. She would let the silence in. Maybe as the waves approached, the angels would help her empty the pockets. Maybe the moon and stars would call her to join them, or maybe like the flowers they would incite her to rise up and live.

WHEN AT LAST she left the hospital, she walked aimlessly on the street, in sunshine, feeling her muscles and the heat of the air, then ordered a car. She invented a destination, but in truth there was no place she wanted to arrive at, not even the beach. She confessed her deception to the driver and asked where he thought she should go. The man laughed. He was young and golden and wore his black hair long. His name was Miguel.

"Maybe the desert," she said.

"Which desert?" he asked.

She looked into his eyes, beautiful and dark, waiting for her answer in his rearview mirror.

"Do you know anywhere I can get a job?" she asked.

"What can you do?"

She shrugged. "Anything. Nothing."

She had no reason to live and no reason not to.

Cloudy with a Chance of Rain

The toddler next door is crying. The neighbor on the other side is yelling *fuck*. The temperature has dropped after weeks of relentless record-breaking heat. Our tempers should be sweeter.

All things grow toward the sun.

I don't get depressed, exactly. What I get is the *I-don't-want-to's*.

The heat came back and finally dropped again, and all night at last it rained. In the early morning I could feel the happiness of the plants and the birds. The human world was full of grief. Explosion. Fire. Pandemic. Idiocy at the head of nations. Incompetence or malign intent, no difference for us who live on the ground.

In 2013 or so, I thought the story was that life goes on, human life goes on, no matter what, some humans would still be here, remembering, singing about the dark times. In 2020, I see the illusion that was.

The garden is full of lessons. A big young stag was in the yard this late afternoon, close to the houses, eating from a half-wild mulberry bush. He was not afraid of me but when he moseyed over to the tomatoes, I asked him to go eat knotweed instead. He regarded me long enough to seem to be considering and turned and trotted off, to hide himself in the little copse he knows as his domain. Later I saw him again and went out to the deck to talk to him down the length of the yard as he chomped on peppermint and weeds. When I thought he was getting too deep into the garden I told him once more to go eat knotweed. He stared at me, then scratched his haunches and started back in on the mint. I made a discouraging sound that stopped him (*Anh! Anh-anh!*) and he considered me again for a moment before turning and disappearing through the invasives into the copse. I thanked him as he left.

Maybe the stag understood what I was asking of him and has moved on by now, down the driveway, back to his family, up the hill and far away. (Do not imagine a rustic landscape. These are little row houses, narrow urban yards, a city street lined with cars.) Or he could still be out there, in among the trees, waiting for darkness and a chance to eat from the garden at leisure. I'm willing to share, up to a point. With the squirrels too. They can have the sunflowers. But the tomatoes, dear creatures, the lettuce and kale—all these are mine.

Because I keep a cat I sometimes find a dead animal tucked away somewhere in a room. I notice first the smell, and hoping it's a plant, I check the pots for soggy bottoms. Then I see it. Today it was a mouse, hidden beneath an end table, stuck between angled slats meant for holding books. I recently took the books out, one step in getting organized, six months into pandemic too late.

We are not hypothetical. Our presence here. Some people object to cats as unnatural predators, throwing life out of balance. By the same reckoning, the cat's little rodents are unnatural prey, come out of the woods with us to fill a city, the same as the felines. All here together, invasive as knotweed—beautiful, edible, ineradicable.

In spring there will be strawberries, fertilized with mouse bones.

Pandemic Dreams

THE PROSPECT OF meeting a man who, if all went well, might someday become her second husband exhausted Caroline so completely that she canceled their internet-match-made Zoom date and, to satisfy her senses, went to bed with a box of chocolates and the bouquet of lilacs she'd ordered days before. She still wore her pearl necklace and fingered the pendant while deciding whether to read or to watch TV. *Seventy-Seven Sunset Strip*, an old show from her mother's childhood, was a possibility. Instead, she chose a song, also from her mother's childhood era, Janis Joplin belting out "Me and Bobby McGee." It occurred to her, as the pearl grew warm in her hand, that she might be missing her mother, who long ago had left her when she left her father for a man named Easton and visions of life on a beach. On the silent television a commercial popped up, a turquoise pool and a tropical grove. Caroline wanted to know something, she didn't know what. She gripped the pearl and sucked on a chocolate that melted in her mouth. She wondered about the man she had decided—even though their date would have been virtual—not to meet. His name was Allston. What sort of name was that, she asked herself, and realized it was a name not unlike the name of the man who had taken her mother away so long before. Who would Allston have turned out to be? Someone like that man who took her mother? The song ended and before another could begin she raised the volume on the television and yanked the necklace off her neck. She listened to the pearls land and rattle and roll across the floor. The lilacs made her sneeze.

THE AIR IS cool but not fresh, something stuck and stagnant lingering around dead trees and ruins of whatever human thing had stood here, stones and beams and firepits, moss covered, buried, impossible to read.

I don't know what to do, says a man whose face she doesn't recognize but seems to know. I don't know where to turn.

I can't help you with that, she says.

A cow grazes on the hillside, several cows, thin lumbering creatures, scrawny silhouettes against a setting sun.

In the morning he rolls up a steel door that protects bodega windows.

A cat strolls near as he hoses down the sidewalk.

You can help me, he says. You know the answer. I know you do. You hold the key. I have to believe it.

Rain begins to fall, unexpectedly, and he quickly shuts off the hose.

Clouds are gathering, darkening the heather, the barrens, the stones of the ruins beginning to glisten.

The cat follows him into the empty store and hops up onto the counter, asking for a treat. He scratches its ears and turns on the radio.

You can believe it if you want to, she says. But it isn't true. You might do better to investigate why you can't let go of that view.

Rain isn't yet falling, but the smell of rain fills the mist beginning to roll, visible, in the wind. As if time is moving backward.

The cows wander, suddenly, spooked by something unknowable — a person, a gust, a flash, the cry of a bird.

You've had the answer all along, he says. You told me you did. You've always —

No, she says. You made that up. That's made-up stuff. I'm just living my life over here.

Crows, a murder of crows, descend out of the clouds, take up residence on the piles of stones, sing to one another and the wanderer and the night, or the morning, or the day.

The news is full of war and devastation.

But I need you, he almost says, before the words die in his heart. She knows it isn't true. He understands it isn't true. Yes, he says then, instead. Yes.

Caw! go the crows. Caw! Caw!

When the rain stops, the cat finds a patch of sunlight in the window and spreads itself out in luxurious relaxation.

CAROLINE HATES HEDGES, those little shiny leaves. She grew up regarding hedges as fences, barriers. She hates barriers and barricades, hates walls and tidy trim. She grew up with tidy trim, gingerbread houses all made of candy, gumdrops and jellybeans and frosting like dead plaster or Elmer's glue. She hates her past — it's clear to her whenever she glances back over a shoulder in that direction — but loves her present life, or her recently present life, the sun, the moon, the stars, the play of hope in the palm trees, the wild youth, the songs, the dance of the ocean's waves. She loves the tacos she buys, or recently bought, on the corner near the office building where she works — recently worked, and hopes to work again before long. She loves the flowers on her desk every day, every day new, flowers from her own garden and the gardens of the people she works with, worked, and will again. She loves the people she works with, etc., or thinks she does, because she has forgotten the many times their words or actions have hurt her, just a little bit or even sometimes a lot. She has forgotten the day Richard in accounting made it clear he would not be interested in going out with her even though he flirted mercilessly for months before she asked him. She has forgotten the beautiful woman he brought as his guest to Caitlin's wedding. She has forgotten how sick she got that night on chocolates and red wine. If she could she would remember why she had cared that way about Richard in the first place, Richard and his beautiful date with her perfect makeup and lavish hair. She would remember more than the phrase "merciless flirting," would remember the way Richard gently touched her elbow at the elevator that first day she noticed him and would remember how back then he always caught her eye in meetings and leadership trainings, how he established the silent bond between them, set it up and opened it, the heat, and the way he whispered in her ear, pushed aside her hair and nearly kissed her there, right at the back of the neck, where she has always, when kissed or vaguely touched or even lightly breathed on, shivered with a delicious chill. She would remember the green of the tie she had given him when she was his secret Santa, a tie he has never worn, the exact green of the paint on her porch back home before her mother left her.

She enjoys the greens here, the green of her lawn and the green ocean and her couch and walls that are a foggy sealike green. She likes green curry and green tacos and the green sauce they give you with papadam at her favorite Indian restaurant, where she hopes to eat again soon. She often wears green dresses these days and green perfume. Green is her color now that she's not in Iowa or Kansas anymore, where all she ever wore was khaki and pink or blue.

She has noticed, though, since leaving all that pink and blue behind, that she sometimes now doesn't know quite who she is, or why, or what, and especially how. How are you? people ask in the morning when she gets to work with her daily flower (asked, got) and, honestly, she knows when she's honest with herself that she doesn't know what to say. She would like to explore this not knowing, if only she could get a handle on how to approach it. She would like to sit down with Richard maybe, or even with Allston, the man she had decided not to meet, and tell him how little she really understands.

In the morning she'll be at work with them again, Richard and

Caitlin and the rest, at work alone in her apartment and for a while, on gallery view, face-to-face—makeup perfect, earrings a-dazzle, silky new green shirt buttoned or un- just so, lilacs visible over her shoulder in the little rectangle that represents herself.

How's everyone doing?

BECAUSE THE RAIN smells of sulfur, we wait at the window before going out. We aren't sure what we'll find out there, luminous puddles, quavering jellyfish, stinking steam. The children are the first to see the chicken, pecking around outside in the pooling rain, followed by a scrawny dog, hunting the chicken maybe, afraid to strike.

Save the chicken! one of the children shouts, and soon they all take up the cry.

We're unsure what to do. We know it's dangerous out there and we don't trust the rain. It confuses us. We have not seen rain in such a long time.

Save the chicken! the children are crying, until one of them crawls out the window and into the wet.

Her T-shirt soaks through in minutes but she scoops up the chicken and raises her face and drinks. The hungry dog whimpers, following at her heels as all three clamber in through the window.

The children laugh, and we, the grownups, admit that we feel embarrassed, even ashamed.

The dog flops down on the rug by the fire, still whimpering, until another of the children goes to sit with it and rubs its ears, spreading a wild wet doggy scent throughout the room. The girl who rescued the chicken keeps it clutched to her wet T-shirt while one of us gets her a cup of hot cider.

We watch as she drinks and wonder, all of us, about the rain, the window, gazing out again, curious about the chicken and the wet earth crawling maybe with living things that we can no longer believe in. We have not known rain for so long. We don't trust the rain and don't know what to do about the danger. We've forgotten even what the danger is, although we understand something of the urgency of the children wanting to save the chicken. We know, without knowing how, that the danger was not the feral dog, and we are afraid of our ignorance and forgetfulness, and afraid of our children. Luminous puddles, quavering jellyfish, stinking steam are nothing compared to this, our own not knowing.

We wait at the window, smelling the sulfur, afraid to stay, afraid to leave, not knowing anymore why, or what anything out there means.

YES, THERE HAD been a husband, married when they were both too young. Yes, Caroline had left him; left the way her mother left, if not exactly; left Kansas for Iowa, to leave without moving at all far away. Ambivalent even then. Now, because of the pandemic, she sometimes wonders how he is, but holds off calling, writing. She had not wanted to leave him, not really, but had wanted to be free of the constant fear that he would leave her. She had even recognized that the fear arose from her own mother's abandonment, but knowing this hadn't helped her, had just made her husband's eventual departure all the more obvious and inevitable.

She tortured herself, until like her mother she escaped.

She thinks of him fondly these days, even sometimes with desire. He's married again, happily, and a father, probably all cooped up together now in a not quite big enough house, but that husband and father isn't who she thinks of when she thinks of him. Rather she thinks of the boy he had been, long and lean, the force of his hips, his thighs pressing against her. She thinks of his hunger for her, his need for her flesh. She thinks of her body receiving him, and the image of him waiting for her before their first date, leaning against a wall, one long leg bent back against it. She thinks of his dark eyes, his black hair, which was wild in those days, when they were both so young. In those early days she had even worn red sometimes, and gold, and purple. She was another Caroline altogether, just for that little while. She can almost remember her, almost taste her—desired, hungry, gorgeous, fierce—her own lost self.

She almost calls him.

She almost calls Richard.

She almost app-chats Allston.

She dozes. She wakes. She eats another chocolate. She watches another movie and considers, idly, whether, when all this is over, to adopt herself an orphaned cat. She can almost feel it in the bed beside her, where her extra pillow is, a warm living bundle with beating heart and claws.

Cul-de-Sac

Gunman

An idea gets stuck in his head. With each new idea he buys a new gun.

Seven of Nine was his favorite. When he found out who she was in real life he stalked her. Or trolled. Online. Only for a while. Until he got bored and sought out another. She wasn't so young anymore but still gorgeous. Like his mother, who had been a beauty in her time.

Seclusion and restraint have taught him something, or reminded him of what he already knew. Everywhere he looks, signs point to the not-yet-arisen, invisible powers: invisibility becoming visible.

The sun, too, is a star.

He knows himself as the man from someday.

Nothing adds up.

Time, for example. A sidereal day is almost four minutes shorter than the conventional or solar day and the underdog isn't always the good guy.

Underdog today, bad dog tomorrow.

When paralyzed with doubt and dread he likes to shoot a gun. He likes to wrap his hand around it, anywhere, and pump. An equal opportunity shooter.

In another world, or life, he would be a dog, a wolf, or maybe an eagle, a hawk, an owl. Or prey. A vole, a mouse, a mourning dove. Everything possible, in every world but this.

His Grandmother

For a time when she was a child they lived in a house with a fireplace and they sometimes made a fire.

The dream child, underwater, as if asleep, in the bath. An old tub, classic, claw-footed. The sleeping grandma, drifting, cries his name. Later, departing, her son behind her, stopped at a corner: You aren't coming with me? No, the son says. You could have told me, the mother thinks. Or says. The grandmother. She let them drown. The end of a life. Her own. No living left in her. And still her days go on and on.

Follow the shadows, what's moving in the background, or hiding in stillness.

Pandemic winter, in a city without winter.

In the fireplace, they popped corn. They may have roasted apples, on skewers, or sticks. Or maybe she made that part up. Marshmallows, more likely than apples. But apples come first to mind. So long ago. No witness left.

She should have been a lawyer, her mother always said.

Gunman

Today he brought a gun, guns—he had bought another, recently bought several—and a camera with a zoom lens, hanging off his neck and whacking his flabby chest, while down in his quixotic saddlebags, clips and jars of bullets and jam masquerade as art supplies.

The sun is a star that burns the skin. Some people sicken with it, others without. Without, we die. With too much we die. *I am the man from someday.* The sun is a star. That's all you need to know to get how tiny we are, inconsequential.

In another world, or other life, he might have been a doctor, saving lives instead of taking them, respected in his arrogance instead of despised.

A word or a phrase gets lodged in his head and plays-back there forever and ever.

History, written by winners. Victory is truth.

He knows they will be coming for him. Gunning.

Warriors don't make peace.

Carnival

Another woman (not the grandma) watches from her window, hesitating. She will be in the street all day with him (not *him*, another man). Together. They haven't spent this much time together in years, not since his last divorce. He said he would pick her up, and he arrived right on time, out in the street, engine running. He phoned and waved up at her. She wanted to say she was suddenly sick, migraine or flu, the cat had a seizure, a pipe burst—anything to get out of the drive with him, like old times, side by side in a car. But in the old days she had been the driver—he never drove, he didn't know how.

He's proud of it now, this vintage Porsche. "It's forest green," he says, as if she can't see.

What was I thinking? she asks herself, expecting to die, the wind in her hair.

He weaves easily, in and out of traffic, changing lanes at 80 miles an hour as if he has been doing it all his life. And maybe he has. Maybe he had been lying to her, all those years ago and since, about this too, just another piece of evidence to add to the dossier, the case against him that proves he has always been a mistake. From the beginning he had been like this, weaving, changing, trafficking—but in what? His life. All of his life—

The brakes screech and she wakes up from her thoughts, expecting again to die. She can't see—traffic stopped everywhere.

"It's the demonstration," he says. "Already." He gets out and tells her to do the same and pulls up the convertible canvas top and closes the windows and locks the car.

They start walking—she almost doesn't know how and sees that they aren't alone on foot on the freeway, weaving in and out among the cars. What about your car? she wants to ask and can hear him, as if already answering, *I don't like driving anyway*, and almost laughs out loud. At least she isn't in it with him now, side by side.

As they walk down the ramp, he's on his phone, others around them heading for the march too, some in costume, some carrying signs, some raising chants and waving, and she knows she would rather be home watching on her computer screen or the big TV, her windows on the world, instead of out here in it.

When he gets off the phone he says, "We're right on time, roads are closed, we blocked the freeway."

We, she repeats, and wonders who he is this time, the way he changes with every divorce.

Except for this—once more together, as always, this time in the street.

Gunman

He dropped a jar of strawberry jam off the roof and watched it splat and crash on the sidewalk below, the nearest people staring up at him until they got bored with that and made a little eddy circling the broken glass and sticky red stuff that later passersby would ignore or think was blood, while up on his perch he laughs, taking photos and quizzing himself, giving animal names to the people down below: wolf, elephant, jaguar, walrus, vixen—waiting for the doe, the stag, magnificent to shoot.

He is, after all, an artist, and who's to say what kind? Careful, deliberate, functional, gifted, but also jumpy, moody, even paranoid, certainly quirky, wicked, excitable, jazzed on disaster.

When he's old he will be wizened, if he lives so long, but for now he's young, relatively, too young, and agile enough to jump off a roof, twist like a cat and land safely on two feet, agile and young enough to kill (to embrace killing—death—as life) and still to make a visible exit, not quiet or stealthy, and without guilt.

He stands in the zebra crossing and jiggles his pockets, sticks out his tongue, making faces into cell phones and surveillance cameras, lifting a finger, ready to die here and now, to exit, to quit, to lose, or maybe for once to win.

Carnival

In the crowd, another woman (not the grandma, not the woman wishing she had stayed home), a woman named Caroline, edges forward, trying to get closer to the speakers' platform. She doesn't especially want to hear—everything is violently amplified—but she does want to see, not the bigger than life video projections, but the actual human beings, close enough to see their sweat, their actual breathing skin, but the crowd keeps pushing her back, a little shell driven by wave after wave to the shoreline.

She takes shelter from the hot sun under a tiny grove of pepper trees. "Hold on," she says to the man already trying to displace her. "I just got here."

"Room for two," he says, and grins and puts out his hand to shake, then shrugs and offers his elbow, which she also rejects. "Russell," he says.

"Hmm," she says.

Back home she would have taken his hand, would have shaken it warmly. But she isn't in Kansas anymore, hah hah, or in Iowa either, and hasn't been for years, and back home, she thinks, maybe they don't shake hands anymore either.

The man was like a commercial for life insurance. Or deodorant. Or peppermint gum. "You're a pearl," he says.

"A what?" she says.

"Your name. I'm guessing your name is Pearl."

She has to laugh, not genuinely, but not exactly falsely either.

When another wave of the crowd pushes another man into the shade of the trees, "Let's get out of here," Russell says, as if he sees a prospect in her, a customer for his sale.

The scent of anise reaches her from out of the crowd as another wave brings children to them, a boy and a girl carrying lilac boughs, then a wave of white-faced people draped in red. A silence comes with them, as if they are performing. And they are, she sees, and watches, mesmerized and counting, seventy-seven red-robed people, miming chaos and grief. Her irritation at Russell lifts. She accepts a lilac bough from the girl and follows the people in red back out to the sun and into the crowd and up the street.

Gunman

He had been working as a reenactor at Disneyland until the hoax called coronavirus shut everything down. All his life, his life had been stolen from him by hoaxes: when he was a kid the diagnostic cascade that put him on drugs for ADHD, the bomb scares at his high school that kept him from going to college, the WMDs that set in place the chain that dragged him years later to Iraq, the mortgage meltdown that killed his best chance at marriage, the restraining order that cut him off from his one true girlfriend when they were both so young—forced unemployment was nothing different.

You might think he's whining. He's not. Believe it.

Or don't. He doesn't care. He grew up with his grandma, a little bit spoiled.

His father was a petty gangster, and like his father he had conned his way through school. He had always wanted women more than they wanted him, but for a while he had flash and sometimes that was enough for him to get over. Flash and no substance, the girl would say, sooner or later. He had words for women like that. Words he knew were ugly but he didn't care. The words didn't mean anything anymore, not when any random teenager can spew them at strangers and keep on walking. Still, in the intimacy of a bedroom, a hotel room, a janitor's closet, a public dressing room, a toilet stall, those words had a certain force. They left him pleased with himself, even if the rest of his performance gratified himself alone. The other, girl, woman, whatever, didn't matter, not in his world, not then, not now.

As California goes so goes the nation. As always before.

At least to send him to Iraq they had to teach him to use a gun.

By the time it was time to suit up and go back to Fantasyland he had better things to do.

•

Carnival

"I want you all to know what I'm doing here," a small man on the corner shouts in a language that no one parading past him knows or even vaguely recognizes. "You know what I'm doing? I've had it with you people, all of you, with your costumes and your signs and your pink hair and tattoos, your nose rings, fucking nose rings, your red robes and white painted faces, your die-ins in the street, I'll show you a fucking die-in, come to my country and see for yourselves, do some good in the world instead of all this performance, the only gesture you have to offer—do you know what it would take for someone in my country to paint his face white and drape himself in red and make a display in the street, to lie down and pretend to die, when where I come from people are every day actually dying? I'm so fucking over your art and your good intentions, I rage and all I get is more rageful, while you're out here laughing and posing for your pretty pictures, and I would like to just do that with you, I would love my tears to be black makeup painted on white, not seared into the skin—my dead in the street, my hungry and thirsty, my lost and wounded, all real, not paint, and I have no patience now to perform this, my reality, on the hope to wake you and your people up to this actual world. Why, when reality doesn't wake you up, what makes you think performance will? Is that the world you live in? Yes?"

He pauses as if he expects the people passing to have understood his words, to stop and think and answer, until he gives up waiting and answers for them.

"Yes, well, sure it is," he says, a little more—almost—gently, no longer entirely shouting. "Yes, and, okay, maybe it's not your fault, it's not, I know, and maybe it's even true that this peacock display is the only thing your people will ever understand. I don't know, what do I know? I'm a stranger here. Maybe performance is all you have, and not even your dead, your own dead, will ever be able to free you from it. I pity you then. I spit, but I spit with pity."

Gunman

A phrase or a name gets into his head and repeats there forever and ever: Chidi Anagonye, Chidi Anagonye, Chidi Anagonye ...

He sees invisible powers. AstraZeneca. AstraZeneca.

Words from the movie *Snowpiercer*: "the misplaced optimism of the doomed."

The immobilizing fights we used to have.

Living with the virus was like waiting for an extinction event, an asteroid or space junk to hit the earth. Or something up from below. Igneous intrusions. Pick of the litter. Or runt. Bottom of the bag. The barrel. Dead end.

He'll get your sympathy. As if there were no politics. Or maybe not.

Every sun was a star but not every star a sun. What was it that made a sun then—planets in orbit or planets that gave life?

He'll have your sympathy, until he pulls the trigger.

Even so, he asks that you not get him wrong—he isn't hallucinating or hearing voices, reading omens or listening to spirits, he's done his share of acid and that, he knows the difference. He's focused on what's real, verifiable, active in the empirical world of guns and governments, trucks and highways, mountains, rivers, air, water, food.

He grew up with his grandma, a little bit spoiled.

How many suns can there be?

You might think he's whining. He's not. It was what it was. He's studied the magician and seen through his tricks. Seclusion and restraint have taught him what he already knew: the rules are arbitrary, stacked against you forever, and up to him to break.

His Grandmother

She will have done everything. Nothing will have stopped him. She turned him one cheek, then the other. Nothing enough, never for long.

She felt him as an implosion. A sun preparing to collapse on itself, into her, preparing to collapse her.

Shall I say I knew something like this would happen, would have to happen? I didn't know. But something, maybe, did.

He was a demon child. How could such a boy be real? His father too and his grandfather.

She had always been attracted to pretty men, men with skinny hips, roving eyes, restless hearts. Beefy boys did nothing for her.

Gunman

He can't say what he hates. He cannot say that what he feels is hate. He can't say even that he feels. But he knows what he knows.

Nothing can be clearer to him, not anymore.

Life was out of time. The universe of suns was infinite, without time, and if suns are infinite so are we—how can it matter then what happens to us, even to the least of us?

He's thirty-three years old, and it's time to die.

He is, after all, an artist, and he knows how you love the desperado, the rangy guy dressed in black, his eyes, dark and penetrating, his mouth, those fleshy lips, his not-quite-perfect teeth. You love everything asymmetrical about him, the shock of hair that falls to the left across his forehead, the cant of his shoulders, his hips, the tattoos on his fingers, the single earring, the mole, the shiny boots. No matter if your own desperado doesn't fit this description—he doesn't himself, not anymore. Maybe yours is thick-set and shaves his head, wears a heavy beard, tattoos his big freckled biceps, his pot belly. Whether he's black or brown or sunburned or ghastly pale or pink. Whether she's a woman, muscular, bleached, well-endowed. Or they're gender neutral, ethereal or not, forever out of reach. Whatever form they come in. You love the outlaw in any shape because the outlaw is who you want to be. You want to break the rules. As if there were no politics. You want the outlaw to break them for you.

So goes the nation.

He has your sympathy until he pulls the trigger.

Maybe even after, depending on what he kills.

His Grandmother

At Halloween they floated apples in a bucket of water and tried to catch them with their teeth. Did they really do this or is it just an image of a thing someone once upon a time created to stand for autumn in a part of the world alien to the place where she has always lived? She can see the red sticky glaze of a candied apple, but did she ever eat or even touch such a thing? The first apple she remembers is brilliant and poisoned, made to put a beautiful girl to sleep forever, gift from a jealous queen disguised as a harmless old woman.

This was make-believe, of course, animation, the first movie she ever saw, in a drive-in, she thinks, in memory the apple glittering, crimson and enormous on a hot starless sky.

The city braces for another heat dome.

He was a beefy boy. How did he get a hold on her?

He was a beefy boy. Make sense of that.

Pack Rat, All Will Be Well

EDDIE'S ADULT CHILDREN thought he had become a pack rat and didn't hesitate to tell him so, voicing their alarm as he filled his second bedroom with carefully packaged collections of objects that other people routinely recycled or threw away—things he would have stored in the basement, if he'd had a basement, if he had lived anywhere with a basement since leaving Xenia, Ohio, so many years ago.

His collecting was a protest against a world of waste, he said.

Only his grandson Harry understood.

Harry loved to help him sort and label and imagine future uses for jars and plastic tubs, egg cartons and rubber bands, packing materials, plastic bags, knives, forks, spoons, straws—*My God, straws*, Eddie thought.

Sometimes they found a use, a kindergarten that wanted his egg cartons, an artist who wanted his rubber bands or plastic straws, once even a kennel that had a need for the big white buckets he collected from restaurants where he made friends with anyone willing to pass their empty treasures on to him.

Cecilia, Harry's babysitter the last few years, very young and bouncy and inventive with her hairstyles and jewelry and painted nails, once took all of Eddie's plastic bags and utensils to make a Halloween costume, a flouncy gown and jewels and tiara. She sprayed the whole getup purple and silver and won a prize.

But his sons and daughters couldn't see it.

They had lived in the sprawling city their whole lives. Eddie and his wives, first and second, were all from somewhere else, places the sons and daughters would never know and would never understand. The sons and daughters had grown up here and become something other and left him and their mothers behind. Their lives from the beginning had been bright and meticulous and after so many decades they had no use for their father's orderly collecting of scrap and waste. In their brightness they didn't recognize his collections as anything but trash, his frugal care as anything but an old man's fretting and fussing, his own meticulous concern for overburdening the environment as anything but eccentricity, maybe even the onset of dementia. They saw aberration, a problem to be ignored or worried over, and in either case hidden.

How had he raised such sons and daughters, who had eyes only for what was shiny and new? What new thing would they ever find that could hold a candle to Cecilia's purple plastic dress, shaped and stretched and painted and polished with love to simulate satin and silk, her crown of radiant forks, her necklaces and bracelets alchemized from plastic spoons? Cecilia understood him. Even so young and bouncy and nothing at all like his own children, she was willing to join him in collecting his potential treasures and helped him find the people who would value them and take them and use them. Cecilia had found the kindergarten and the artist and the kennel—although she confessed to Eddie later that the kennel had been unhappy with the buckets. He wondered about that, asking Harry what the problem could have been, until they were fabulating misadventures set off by the dogs' catching a whiff of peanut butter, say, or sauerkraut, lingering in the hard white plastic.

Harry insisted that just because maybe the people at the kennel didn't appreciate their protest against the world of waste, any more than his own parents and aunts and uncles and cousins did, his grandad shouldn't lose heart. He, Harry, would always be here to help, along with Cecilia, and the next time there was a climate demonstration or an Earth Day parade they would make a big float and call it *The Pack Rat* and Cecilia would paint a giant plastic banner celebrating Eddie's collection. A beautiful photo would go viral after appearing in the *L.A. Times* and Eddie's adult children and their wives and husbands, including Harry's mother and father, could eat their hearts out.

EDDIE'S NEXT-DOOR NEIGHBOR on the west was a woman who lived alone and rarely greeted him, or greeted him coldly, even though they had lived side by side the entire two decades since he'd moved in, not long after Sharon died. He thought the neighbor was schoolmarmish, when he thought about her at all. Still, without thinking of her, he felt her there, uneasily, half-consciously. Having come to live in this city as a young man, he had grown accustomed to the climate, with its five herky-jerky seasons—rain, fog, sun, wind, fire—and its longer pulse of drought and flood; got used to the distances he had to drive, even to get to a supermarket for apples and a loaf of bread; embraced the end of solitude that came with his first marriage and in time accepted the finalities when Simone left him and again when Sharon died; he had taken in stride the explosions that were his children when they were young and by now had reconciled himself to their rare and ever more random presence. But in twenty years alone in this house he had never grown accustomed to this neighbor.

(Deirdre was aware of him over there, the tall, thin old man on the other side of the not-so-high hedge that ran between their lawns. She would stand on her porch in the early mornings and listen to birdsong or in the afternoons to the voices of children as they scattered up the street after school. At times a morning was so quiet she imagined she could hear the ocean. She couldn't, but on certain damp or windy days she could smell it, the sea all around her, wrapping her tenderly, the embrace of a mother, or a child. The old man next door, she thought, was morose, taciturn. She thought of him as a scarecrow and liked to greet him, to challenge him to speech or a wave or a smile. She was so used to his refusals that she didn't notice how icy her own greetings had become.)

Although he had no idea what her name really was, Eddie saw as he watched her—not every day or every week but year after year—that as she aged she became almost regal, and he had begun to think of her as Elizabeth Regina. When now and then they had to speak to one another, about trimming the hedge, say, he would buck himself up, force himself to stand tall, incline his head as if to a queen, and stubbornly resist whatever notion she was putting forth. One year she had wanted to trim the hedges into topiary rabbits. He was unyielding. But time was changing him, too. Maybe rabbits wouldn't be so bad. Maybe the schoolchildren would stop and help with the trimming; there were not as many children in the neighborhood as when he came to live here, and those there were didn't seem to know him. Maybe the neighbor would offer him some of the fresh bread he sometimes smelled when she baked. Maybe they would even go for a drive together, to the ocean or a park. It was a long time since he had enjoyed the company of a woman. Cecilia, still a child, didn't count.

He watched the neighbor from his morning window, how she stood straight as an arrow on the porch of her little blue house and breathed.

DEIRDRE HAD AWAKENED that morning from a dream in which she found herself back in time, in the bedroom of her childhood, hiding in darkness and silently saying to her childhood self, "Be brave and live your own life." Together the words, the room, the longing filled the waking moment with tears until she roused herself to begin her morning ritual:

make the bed, brush the teeth, take the first round of vitamins, do ten minutes of tai-chi warm-ups, dress, read the day's devotional reflection, then go outside to stand on the porch and breathe.

She knew her scarecrow neighbor was watching and she noticed that his watching felt different to her in this moment, perhaps because of the sensitive aura still lingering from the dream. The morning devotion she had read, written by Julian of Norwich, a medieval Christian recluse, also lingered, infused with her own mood:

> And I saw that nothing hindered me but sin. And I thought if sin had not been, we should all have been clean and like to our Lord as he made us. But Jesus in this vision answered and said, "Sin is needful, but all shall be well. And all shall be well. And all manner of thing shall be well."

Be brave and live your own life, she heard—repeated from out of the dream. She wanted a cigarette. She had not smoked in thirty years. An odd wish, then. A deflection. When it had come time to live her own life, when she was sixteen, seventeen, she had started smoking instead. Like that honey-colored girl she saw so often next door, sitting on the front porch, texting or whatever on her phone. Such a creature of the decade, with her black snaky curls, her dangly earrings, her cropped black pants and heavy boots. Her face a vision of innocence and hybrid beauty. Maybe that girl would not make the same mistakes that Deirdre herself had made. Or the boy the girl brought to play with his grandfather.

Deirdre had not known her own grandfathers. Or her grandmothers. She had grown up without elders in her life, her parents all but children themselves. Now she was one of the old and solitary. It was hard sometimes to comprehend. What this life had come to. She had always had grit, she thought. An ability to learn, to grow, by making effort. An ability to value failure. After a rocky start—she had been something of a hippie, psychedelic drugs, the open road, revolution, free love, and all—with patience and perseverance she had built a little life; yet despite the willingness to fail, she had not learned to plan for misfortune, and time and again misfortune had caught up with her. First the parents, which was to be expected, then the husband, then their son. She was the only one left now and had been alone the entire new century, which was now no longer new. The former century seemed today almost not to have existed, especially from the vantage of these last few years, with their near reversal of every good thing she'd taken for granted as accomplished.

Except on a morning like this one that started with a haunting dream, the old century faded into its own never-neverland, as far from her present as the anchorite of Norwich. And still, Deirdre instructed herself, *All shall be well, and all shall be well, and all manner of thing shall be well.*

WHAT HARRY AND Cecilia had in mind was to construct a blue Antarctic glacier and a sky of brilliant southern lights on a flatbed they would set up in Eddie's driveway, using his trove of plastics as materials, until the night before the parade, or demonstration or whatever, they would add huge blocks of ice. They wanted to dress themselves up as penguins or huskies or maybe a seal and a Chilean snow queen (because one of Cecilia's abuelitas had left childhood and her own abuelas in Chile almost fifty years before to travel north, first to Mexico, and then to California, newly married, with her Mexican husband, Cecilia's old abuelo, who no longer walked this earth). They would gather a crowd to join them and all together they would march or ride the float and sing "people have the power" and "el pueblo unido jamas sera vencido," blowing bubbles and throwing white flowers and ice shavings and bits of plastic cut and painted into little fishes dying in the heat and sun. The concept kept changing, detail by detail, except for the songs, until the glacier was a rain forest and they were throwing plastic butterflies, and then they wanted the float itself to go through that metamorphosis and in a grand finale the fish and butterflies and Itzpapalotl herself to come alive.

Cecilia brought Eddie a thirty-page document she had printed off the internet, "The Authoritative Guide on How to Build a Float," full of technical illustrations and diagrams of trailer and flatbed construction. No way he was renting or buying or building that, from scratch or otherwise.

He liked the costumes, though. He liked the plastic glacier and the butterflies and especially he liked the songs. He would buy a guitar, he told them. So Harry could learn to play and they could practice their singing with an instrument. Maybe he would even join in. He did a little research online and talked them into a walking float—no flatbed, no truck, no fossil fuels—just their bodies, their music and costumes and props, manifesting their vision solely through performance. He saw Cecilia at first resist and watched as moment by moment her opposition turned, until in the end you'd have thought the idea was her own.

Even without the flatbed there were props and banners and landscapes to construct, a glacier, a rain forest, their play and routines to develop—not only the songs to practice, but Cecilia's brother and sister

71

and her friends and Harry's and even his cousins, Eddie's other grand-children, to recruit and choreograph as musicians and singers and stage-hands and dancers.

They didn't know yet what occasion would bring their production out from under his carport into the heart of the city, into the streets. They would just have to be ready, Cecilia said. They would know the call when it came.

EDDIE'S NEWER NEIGHBOR, on the east, sat in her driveway, separated from his by a narrow strip of geraniums the color of sockeye salmon. The carport was still a sore point—not that it was Eddie's fault. Agnes understood that the structure had been added to the property already, years before he'd bought his otherwise mirror-image house. But the carport cast its shadow over the geraniums most of the afternoon, and Agnes had begun to wonder what she could plant in their place that would be as brilliant in color and happier in shade. She had once tried talking with him about taking the carport down. He was almost willing, he said, but opposed to destruction and waste. Typical, she thought. He was an old man, after all. She wondered what she was doing in this neighborhood full of old people. She would become one of them, living here alone. She should be sharing an apartment in Los Feliz or Lincoln Heights or a little condo in Santa Monica. Someplace with bars and a metro stop. As if she could afford such a place. And she embraced the quiet of this neighborhood, the privacy. Nobody got in her business here. Nobody got in her face, expecting her to be someone she wasn't. They left her to herself. Friendly, but only just. She had finally settled on a life, a reliable job, or career, whatever, and now a home of her own to hide in.

She was stalling, sitting in the driveway, sat there long enough to contemplate the party developing over at Eddie's: long-haired mixed-race children and Latinx teenagers and art-making and music. She was of mixed grand-parentage herself, French and Vietnamese, mostly Viet-namese. She had been lost for a while, she knew, drifting from one thing to another, one lover to another, woman to man and back to woman, and once even, a mistake, a girl just out of high school. She was at her best in solitude. She had that in common with the old people. Now suddenly this fiesta was developing next door. It reminded her of New Orleans, the year-round preparations for carnival. She had left celebration behind with Katrina when she came alone to California to make a new start.

Trading hurricanes for earthquakes and fire, twenty years old and a refugee like her parents.

Stalling still. She hated working crowds. Crowds meant trouble, sometimes even disaster. Solitary violence was easier to reckon with—after a brutality, the silent voice that says *I live.*

DEIRDRE HEARD THEIR street music almost every day now, Saturday and Sunday mornings and every late afternoon, a band and chorus of many instruments and many voices growing week by week. Tattooed rappers, male and female, black and brown and gold and pinkish white. Boys wearing fedoras playing Andean melodies on wooden flutes. Dancers in red and feathers, beating drums. The young grandson with a guitar, shouting off-key while the beautiful honey girl carried their tune. When they weren't singing or making music they worked together on some sort of project, constructing what began to look like a platform, long poles of bamboo resting on upended buckets, extending back toward the garage and out toward the street. She saw what might have been palm trees or banana plants, a monkey made of plastic bags, painted butterflies dancing on rubber-band strings. She knew they must be rubber bands from the way they bounced. When one day the boy and the girl and their companions were painting rainbows, big ones, little ones, rainbows of unusual colors and combinations, suddenly she wanted very much to join them, a song running through her head, "Lucy in the sky . . ."

When the rains came, the children—that's what they were, all of them—covered the platform and everything on it with blue tarps as protection from water blowing in from the open sides of the carport, and from then on for a time lights came on every afternoon in the garage, where her neighbor no longer parked his car. Deirdre missed hearing them sing. She missed watching whatever magic they were making out there unfold. She became impatient for the rains to end. Maybe she would finally go and speak to them. Maybe she would not wait for an invitation, which after all was unlikely to come. Maybe she would bake some bread—many loaves of bread—and carry them over in her big summer basket, just knock on the door or ring the bell.

EDDIE SMELLED BAKING bread long before he saw her. It was late morning on a day without rain, and Cecilia and the kids would not arrive for hours. He was staring at the newspaper, sunk into a reverie the smell of baking bread evoked. Simone used to bake when he and she were young and poor together, and the aroma of yeast wafting in through open windows awakened an image of his first son and daughter as toddler and kindergartener thrusting pudgy hands out while Simone buttered slabs of steaming bread. The son was a banker now and the daughter a minor executive at a vast international trading firm. She spoke in terms like "stranded assets" and "diversified portfolio," but Eddie had never understood what the company actually traded in. It was their stepfather who had reprogrammed them toward business, their stepfather and an unrecognizable Simone. Their children too, his grandchildren, were heading in the same direction, or had seemed to be, until they started joining their youngest cousin on weekends at Grandpop's to make music and a parade.

It was a relief to Eddie. He wanted to love all his children and grandchildren equally. But their lives had become so alien to his, and not only their lives, but their convictions. They lived in a completely other world. He had considered himself a socialist as a young man, and at heart he still did. Simone had been a devotee of Angela Davis. Then she went to law school and won some awards and had a big student loan debt to pay off and the next thing he knew she was in bed with corporate America. Even so, now and then, he got a glimpse of the Simone he remembered, despite the perfect makeup and straightened hair, in her eyes the old mischief, the troublemaker, the fearless young woman who sang with him and danced. He had to admit he still loved that young person, all vinegar, fire, and hope, so innocent not to have known what she would be willing to become. It turned him sad, then, to think of her—what it must be like to have separated herself so utterly from that spirit of her youth.

Then the doorbell rang. He hadn't seen the neighbor coming and here she was. Not since the topiary rabbits had she stood at his door. He almost greeted her as Elizabeth, before remembering that this was not her actual name. What was her name?

She smiled at him and held up a basket, covered in a blue checkered cloth, its contents unmistakable. "I thought you and the children might like some homemade bread," she said.

She was a tiny woman, up close. Pale and fair, blue eyed. Deirdre, he remembered suddenly. She had been a librarian before she retired. There had been a dog when he first moved here. Black and long haired. Maybe a cocker spaniel? Or something bigger.

He invited her in. He offered her coffee, butter and jam.

Her bread was delicious.

"What are you building out there?" she asked.

He had long taken her for a Republican. Maybe a climate denier. Probably not a Trumper—much too polite. Still, he didn't know how best to answer her question. What if she lodged a complaint? What if he and the kids were breaking some neighborhood ordinance or other that only someone like her would know? Their project had grown too big over the weeks, louder, more visible. Would it grow even bigger when the rains stopped, not just for a day, but until the next year? When they worked outside again in the driveway? When school let out for summer and they went into final production? What if even his room full of carefully catalogued waste went somehow against her notion of the law? She might be like his children, call him a crazy old man. Or worse.

She was waiting for his answer.

"You should ask the children," he said, hoping delay would bring him confidence.

SHORTLY BEFORE CHRISTMAS a memorial parade for the thousand homeless people who had died in the county throughout the year became an angry protest at City Hall, and Agnes, standing at attention, maintaining order, regretted again, not for the first time, having transferred away from the beach. She had always hated crowd control. The move followed from buying the house. The commute was better, had been her reasoning. The other differences she could handle; a body was a body, after all, whatever its condition, wherever it showed up, but these public uprisings and angers set her on edge.

Even before the crowd let loose its outrage, she had been uneasy, haunted by the too familiar drum and trumpet and keyboard, Mardi Gras beads and all. "Death by neglect" the mourners' banner read, with photos and silhouettes and names of the dead. Then just as they started shouting, "Three a day! Too many!" she saw in the crowd the faces of children she recognized from the carport and driveway next door. She wondered if they would know her in her uniform. Probably they would see just another cop.

Still, she did what she could to keep in shadow, to avoid their line of sight. The parade was meant to be a ceremony, not a demonstration. If there was any difference now or ever had been. But crowds were unpredictable and even when peaceful attracted trouble. Shooters liked crowds. So many easy targets, so many personal shields. She wanted the rain to return, to drive the parade on its way, but the sun relentlessly shone. From the darkness where she stood, as she glanced at the children — the honey girl, the brown grandson, the tall blacker boy between them, raising a fist with the crowd — she tried to un-see the phantom crosshairs suddenly trained and shimmering on his singular and brilliant young face.

A few days later the rain came back with a winter storm that flooded roads and triggered accidents, felling an occasional tree, one big eucalyptus smashing flat a famous actor's Audi, an aged California live oak crushing a bicycle delivery boy under its massive trunk.

She would take nature over people any day, even at its most destructive.

AS THE NEW year arrived and settled in and the briefly heavy storms gave way to drizzle and fog, Deirdre often thought about inviting Eddie over for coffee. She had reached the age, she suspected, when a woman becomes invisible. She had waited her whole life to reach this age, its invisibility both resisted and desired. Small as she was, she felt gravity now, changing her form almost beyond recognition, pulling her earthward, although she knew the effects of this gravitational pull couldn't yet be seen. Her mind, too, maybe, was pulling earthward — she wanted to be seen, wanted Eddie, that old scarecrow, no older than she was most likely, to see her.

"I was sitting in a cafe one afternoon," she told him, "when the deep bright burnt-orange red of a shop across the street, which was otherwise just outside the frame of vision, struck with such force and beauty that tears stung the back of the eyes. I have no explanation. When I checked later, I found the shop was a patisserie, a bakery trying to be French. The color had no meaning, no particular psychological or personal association. It just was. Absolute."

"You speak in paragraphs," Eddie observed.

"Maybe so," she said. "I spend too much time alone. I'm sorry."

"No, not at all. Don't apologize. It's rare. Do you listen to NPR? Every day they deliver sentences in which the verbs agree with the object of some preposition instead of with their subjects."

"*The President's impeachment and Biden's latest gaffe continues to dominate the news?*"

"Yes, that too," he said. "And *information about the impacts of donations are available.*"

"*By 2060, the habitability of big parts of developed America are genuinely on the table?*"

"Exactly," he said, and she saw he thought he had found a kindred spirit. "This new one," he said, "have you heard it—*as disastrous than?*"

"*There has never been as honest a President than me?*"

"And *who-* and *whomever*, the distinction erased and their usage governed as if by some rule of sound—"

He seemed about to go on but cut himself short. "What kind of person rants about grammar when the whole world is burning?"

"Yes," she said. "What kind?"—taking care not to plunge into stories of her own life, her wild youth followed by work as an archivist, the box of family genealogies collected by a grandmother she'd never known, the parents dead, the husband, the son—the end of a line.

"I'm—I was—a mechanical engineer," he said. "I started with Hughes but mostly I worked for Disney."

"One robot on the moon, then thousands in the movies?"

She realized she expected he would laugh only when he didn't.

Instead he sat there stopped, as if for a moment she baffled him.

When he found his bearings he said, "Despairing over grammar's a curse I got from my father. He was a newspaperman. He dwelt on what was lost. Now the language loses meaning for other reasons. What's happening here is something deeper than grammar."

"But what?" she asked when he'd stopped again and sat looking at her in silence.

"I don't know," he said. "Something I can't get hold of."

She wanted to reach out a hand to him. She wanted to look him in the eye without turning away. But he was already gazing over her shoulder, out the window toward his driveway, where she imagined the kids were beginning to gather.

THE RAIN DIDN'T last or the fog either. Soon the sky was blue again, bluer than before, and the noisy pageant returned to the carport. But not for long. A rapidly spreading and sometimes deadly virus threatened to become a global pandemic, and overnight, it must have seemed to anyone not paying attention, the city began to shut down. When schools closed and the kids still showed up in the driveway, Agnes wondered as she watched whether it was on her to intervene. She was off duty and the kids were being careful—not touching one another or standing too close, obeying all the guidelines. They even had Purell out there and used it before and after they handled anything and before they went into the house. They did go into the house, now and then, one at a time, probably to use the bathroom, and when now and then Eddie came out, the kids stood even farther from him than from one another, respectful of his age and demographic vulnerability. Better than the assholes hanging out defiantly in bars or partying in their houses, in their carports and garages, falling all over each other, grabbing, fighting, toking, puking, posting videos of chains of human contagion, sharing bottles and joints and kissing, raising hell and proud of it, as if the crisis was one big joke. Parties like those, she enjoyed breaking up. But these kids were different. They took care of one another and they took care of Eddie. And she didn't want them to know who she was, what she did, what her living was.

When she was new here, when Eddie asked, she had answered that she worked for the city, making it clear from her manner that she didn't intend to say more, and saw from his that he heard her and wouldn't ask again. It wasn't easy now to see him as vulnerable. He stood out there as tall and straight-edged as if he had a stick across his shoulders and a ramrod up his back. He was not bent over, not stooped like other old men, not, apparently, frail, but he was old, just the same, and when the woman from the other side came out of her house and joined everyone, she made herself vulnerable, too. Maybe at greater risk than Eddie was. She stood a little closer, as if she had forgotten, or maybe to show that she wasn't afraid. She looked always on the verge of reaching out, of touching—someone, anyone, anything.

When the governor's orders got stricter—nonessential businesses to close, everyone not working in an essential sector to stay home except to buy groceries or walk or run for exercise, always maintaining the minimum six feet of distance, no groups of any size to gather anywhere, not in a public park or outside a private residence—finally most of the kids stopped appearing. And still Agnes saw the girl and the grandson making music under the carport or talking with Eddie from ten feet away.

At first the two old people took turns shopping for one another, Eddie for the woman, the woman for him. They unloaded shopping bags. Each went into the other's house. In it together, Agnes decided. She thought she would like to offer to help. But as a frontline worker, for all she knew, she could be a carrier, infected herself. She was relieved when she began to see food arriving, delivered in boxes, and Eddie and the other neighbor no longer driving off in their cars. She caught herself watching over them, worrying until she caught sight of one or the other or the two together, out for a walk in the evening, the woman wearing a bandanna on her face and Eddie a pirate's skull-and-crossbones on what looked like a homemade mask.

"TRY SHOWING THEM this," Deirdre said, referring to his grown children and their complaints about his pack rat tendencies, and opening to an early page in the book she had been reading during their many days of isolation, read aloud now for him:

"Pack rats build nests out of sticks and stones and bones and urinate on them; the liquid hardens like amber, preserving pack rat nests as if pressed behind glass. A great many of the animals and plants that lived at the time of ancient pack rats later became extinct, lost forever, saved only in pack rat nests, where their preserved remains provide evidence not only of evolution but of the warming of the earth. A pack rat nest isn't like the geological record; it's more like an archive, a collection, gathered and kept, like a library of old books and long-forgotten manuscripts, a treasure, an account of the antiquities of the animals and plants."

Eddie laughed. "We're meant for each other then," he said, without thinking—she had been a librarian, an archivist, a collector like him—and felt his face burn hot. Flushed, as if he had a fever. He didn't, was just embarrassed for himself, for his boyish take on what she was offering. She looked embarrassed, too. For him. More flustered than embarrassed. She remained a mystery.

He changed the subject. "Next door," he said. "Do you think she's a doctor? Maybe a nurse? She works for the city. Maybe she's in public health. Or a social worker. She still goes out almost every day. At all hours. Maybe we should serenade her."

Deirdre didn't answer, but closed her book. "You could read it to them," she said again. "Maybe it would help them appreciate your effort."

"I'm not preserving anything," Eddie said, suddenly cranky.

"Oh, but you are," Deirdre said. "Through transformation. This beautiful, ungraspable—" she struggled for a word—"Rube Goldberg machine the kids are building—"

"If they ever get to meet again—"

"Don't be glum. It's evolving with the time we're living through. It's a theatrical production, made of many moving parts. Or a juggernaut. Jagannatha. Like this virus. Ready to crush us under its wheels. Or with its crown."

He couldn't follow the turns and inconsistencies of her mind. As soon as he caught up with her she had moved on to someplace else.

Just like the world, he thought.

THE WEATHER GOT hot for a while then cool again, a cool that would have been warm in the rest of the country—most of the rest, but not in New Orleans, and Agnes allowed a rare wash of homesickness to pass through her. The lockdown continued, despite gestures toward easing. The days lengthened and the air got dry and the sun and deep blue sky brought heat and wind and fire and the state began to open. Then in Minneapolis four policemen murdered a man, holding him on the ground for eight minutes and forty-six seconds and blocking interference while the officer in charge bore down with his knee with all his weight on the man's neck until he died. And maybe even after. George Floyd. One man. One Black life. The nation watched the video and counted the minutes and seconds, and all over the country, and around the world, lockdown or no lockdown, people poured into the streets to say enough.

Temperatures shot up. Every shift was crowd control, some days quieter than others. Agnes stood on the line or directed traffic or escorted arrestees. Sometimes she listened to speeches and eulogies for the dead. *Blessed are the peacemakers*, somebody said. Her mind went along with the chanting. She wondered how Thomas was doing now, her partner at the beach, who was young and Black and kind and whom she had been sorry to leave. Thomas had always been kind, in every circumstance, gentler than anyone she worked with now downtown. He had cultivated a quiet crush on her, she thought, a gentle crush, and no one at the beach had ever called her cunt or dyke or gook. Not to her face and not behind her back. It was a different culture there, she thought. Or she had just been lucky. Or oblivious, lulled by seaside breezes and the humid, lambent air. For all she knew, Thomas had been looking out for her, just as she looked out for him. Maybe they had worked in a bubble, protected from the men around them, and even the women, by that glaze of innocence that everyone, themselves included, accepted with the paycheck and the uniform.

The days got hotter. After announcing that he wouldn't, the mayor asked the governor to call up the National Guard to protect stores from looting, and the presence of the guardsmen also helped subdue the trigger-happy among the so-called men in so-called blue. The protestors trusted the guardsmen more than they did her uniformed brothers and sisters, eager as some of them were to lob tear-gas cannisters and press onward in military formation into a crowd, wielding clubs and pepper spray, safe behind their heavy shields.

Under blooming jacarandas the people filled the streets with home-made signs and endless chanting. Call: *How do you spell racist?* Response: *LAPD.* One morning church bells rang throughout the city, led by the Cathedral of Our Lady of the Angels. Eight minutes and forty-six seconds of tolling bells.

For you, Agnes thought.

She belonged on the street, with the protestors.

She searched their faces above the masks, their eyes and hair, their clothes and posture and gesture, for the kids from next door.

"I THINK SHE'S a cop," Cecilia said.

"Nah," Kevin said. "Too hot."

Kevin was Harry's seventeen-year-old rock star cousin, and even though she was a year or even two maybe older, Cecilia didn't like him thinking of the neighbor as hot. Not that he was really a rock star, not even a musician. He just had the attitude and swagger and long legs and an aura of some kind of magic, like he knew he would be somebody, and already was.

"OK, boomer," she said, which in the moment definitely made sense, and she wasn't about to defend herself for using a dead ageist expression to challenge a sexist leer. She enlisted Harry to explain.

Kevin wasn't the brightest bulb, she decided, no matter how dazzling he flashed.

The other kids were late, which was annoying, because they had a plan. Many of them had been in the streets for BLM protests after the killing of George Floyd, and some had even marched and made music as far back as the homeless memorial—so many worlds or lifetimes past. For a few weeks they'd gone in small groups to Friday climate strikes, sometimes in costume or with their instruments, to get comfortable with being visible and to practice with an audience and unrehearsed participants, preparing for a big event to come. Then the strikes got canceled because of covid. Cecilia had wanted to launch their full performance on Earth Day, but as Earth Day approached and the city was still locked down, they were out of practice, and Eddie said that even if the stay-at-home order did get lifted, they weren't ready. To her own surprise she didn't argue with him, but when the day came gathered a small group to meet down-town, everyone masked and carefully keeping six feet of distance, and up until the moment when a policeman came and told them to break it up, they were drawing too much of a crowd, they had a good time singing and chilling and dancing, and signing people up to train with them by Zoom for the celebration demonstration that eventually would come.

One of her new recruits that day was a puppeteer who offered to help them make marionettes and dress them and dance them from their hands and fingers on strings. "Cool," Cecilia said and blushed at herself and at the puppeteer's beautiful hands, which he was using to demonstrate on air the moves he could teach them. That night she tried to imagine his mouth, his chin. He was seriously older than Kevin, with dark skin and tight longish curls and gorgeous big black eyes, and shining—definitive-ly a star. She was sure he would never swagger or pitch attitude, at her or any woman, and when they met unmasked on Zoom a few days later, he was even more handsome and radiant than she'd dreamed.

With the puppeteer's online guidance, all summer long she and Harry had been constructing large marionettes, using only (or mostly, if she was honest) waste plastic, rubber bands, bits of string, and papier mâché, dressing them with foil bags and food wraps, matching each costume to the costume she designed for its designated puppetmaster. Harry and Kevin had written skits for the marionettes (mostly Harry, who was ge-nius beyond his age), and now that they could all (at least for a while) meet again in person, Max, the puppeteer, was going to teach the team how to manipulate their creations and work their weird fragile bodies to tell stories.

But the other kids were late, even Max had not arrived, and the air was getting so thick with smoke from the fires in the hills that she and Kevin and Harry decided to wait indoors.

PLANES OVERHEAD, A whistling. Firefighters, Agnes told herself, guessed, or maybe knew—or fresh demonstrations?—but no matter what she guessed or knew, any sound from above would always trigger hypervigilance. On the job, she encountered violence almost every day, or the consequence of violence, and in her flesh, on each occasion, she heard or felt the voice that reminded her she was alive, herself alive, but even so, even when she knew the source of any humming, whistling, droning from the sky, who or what was making it, she—born in Texas, child of refugees, of parents who themselves, though fleeing war, had never lived under aerial bombardment—she, Agnes, withdrew into still-ness and silence to listen for the steady beating of her heart. She knew no other sanctuary, not even one to imagine. Every place she had ever lived had been transformed beyond recognition once she no longer lived in it. Her childhood home in Beaumont, the share house in New Orle-ans, the shelter where she stayed on arrival in L.A., her first apartment in the city, even her second. Flood, hurricane, fire, redevelopment and wrecking ball. She continued to live as if she believed destruction trailed in her wake, even now, even here, in her own secure boxy bungalow with its strip of driveway geraniums.

THE END OF summer, the fall, the early winter, all were dominated by the election and its aftermath, then suddenly a rollout of vaccines. It took Eddie a while to get scheduled even though he was immediately eligible and Deirdre close behind. After a year of being careful, he was in no hur-ry, not enough to get frantic, but once he had a connection to an appoint-ment he was quick to go in. Easy-peasy, he told Harry, even when he was sick for a day after the second dose. Deirdre got even sicker, slept through her 100.5 fever, and as soon as she was well stayed awake and elated for twenty hours straight. Eventually they both evened out and relaxed a little, said to one another that at last they could breathe—grownups were running the country again, and they weren't in imminent danger of a predictably torturous death. A couple of the kids had had the virus, not too seriously, and whenever there was a case the whole crew did a quaran-tine around Eddie and the parade. No one close to him had died, though occasionally he got word of the loss of an old friend or a cousin more distant, back in Ohio or the northeast. Deirdre had heard of the passing of a couple of people from her wild youth and of a former colleague, she told him, but she had been closer, by Zoom, to the death of her brother-in-law and she didn't want to talk about it.

The kids still maintained their pod of sorts and kept up the practice of distance and masks and finally with the weather improving and the virus abating, they gathered once more, and more often, in the driveway to re-hearse, so many of them that Eddie couldn't keep track, watching mostly from the window until it was safe to conduct himself as fully vaxed—and even then, for everyone's sake, he wore one of his skull-and-crossbones masks tight over blue paper-plastic and stood a good six feet away, his heart breaking again at the waste—the probably exponential increase in unrecyclable, unreusable waste the virus had wrought—despite all efforts, his spare room overflowing, a river of packaging plastics, bubble wrap, zipper bags, clamshells, flaccid ice packs—an ocean microcosm.

MAX, IT TURNED out, was not so much older than she was, just twenty-four—but so mature, Cecilia thought—and she was finally almost twenty. She loved his cleverness and the skill of his hands and their touch as he moved with her to demonstrate how to manage the controllers—his long, strong, delicate fingers. She couldn't look at them without imagining, and felt herself blush, grateful for the mask she wore, and his, and embarrassed at her awkwardness with the marionettes that she and Harry and Kevin and the others had spent so many months lovingly creating.

"Don't worry," Max said, and showed her his beautiful patience.

"Maybe I'll leave the dolls to others," she said.

He pretended to be offended but she knew it was a game. She had been teasing him about playing with dolls for months, at first tentatively, feeling him out. She couldn't tell—he was an artist, after all—whether he would even like a girl, a girl like herself, although she did sense in her response to him that there must be something on his side too, and anyhow he knew what she was doing and let her play at it and played along and beyond her, until she could hardly breathe beside him.

"Five years is a big difference," he said to her once. "Bigger than you know. At our age," and she felt he spoke from experience, and she wanted beyond wanting to have that experience with him.

When the Derek Chauvin trial began, they learned with everyone else that Chauvin had kneeled on George Floyd's neck for almost a minute longer than was previously revealed, and when the guilty verdict came in, she went with Max into the street—no marionettes, no music, none of the other kids—just wearing black and kneeling on the pavement with twenty-some other grown-up people, spaced apart and masked, blocking a busy intersection, for the full nine minutes and twenty-nine seconds, silent and still.

Walking back to the car, Max continued the silence, and without thinking about herself, Cecilia reached for his hand. He let her take it. He even smiled, just a little, she could see from his eyes. Tears welled up in her. She didn't know why. What she felt was bigger than she was, bigger than their bodies bearing witness in the intersection, bigger than Max and bigger than Harry and Eddie and whatever they all had been doing for whatever reason all this time.

"I DWELL ON what we're losing," Deirdre said. "Animals and plants—and even more than those lives that are also our lives, the world of uniquely human things—Renaissance palaces of Italy, medieval cathedrals of France, the Alhambra and Fatehpur Sikri, Chichen Itza and the temples at Ankor Wat."

"Bridges," Eddie offered.

"And books," she said, "—all the miraculous books."

"Who will understand them?"

"Who will know their beauty? Who will sing the Magnificat or improvise on a quena or a shakuhachi?" She felt her words' inadequacy. She looked at Eddie, grateful for him, stranger that he was to her, even after this long time-out, longer than any simple year.

"Strangers forever," he said, as if reading her thoughts.

She had spoken of this to him, at some earlier time; she knew there was no magic in it. Still, she appreciated that he remembered and didn't mind showing her. She almost took his hand. She imagined he would have liked her to take his hand. But she was beyond all that. Especially now, she thought, and wasn't sure what this *now* meant to her. She didn't know how to tell him, and almost stood up and left the table, the room, the house, his house.

A widower's house. He was beyond all that too.

"What are we doing?" she said, inadvertently aloud.

"As if we were kids," he said.

"No," she said. "I won't. I'm not. You either."

"You bet," he said.

"I do," she said. She laughed. "I play poker," she said. "Every Friday night. With the boys. These days we play online."

"The boys?" he asked.

"Older even than you. We've been playing for years. My brother-in-law was one of them, before he died."

"Nickels and dimes?"

"Ones, fives, and tens."

"You never told me."

"Never," she said, and laughed at the word, as if they had known one another all their lives.

OUT IN THE driveway Cecilia adjusted her Itzpapalotl headdress, a crown of flames and butterflies. As if magically, everything had come together, every detail perfect beyond anyone's wildest hope. They had rehearsed in public for months, in bits and pieces, in small teams, then alone or in pairs, shut in and online, until, adapting to the possible, in teams again and masked, they had accomplished their final fragmented rehearsals, and now, at last, the day had come when they could walk the whole show together through the streets and help give birth to this march to end all marches, a motley troupe, maintaining distance, vaccinated, masked, dancing loosely in lines then dissolving one after another into the myriad scenes they had given their pandemic year and then some to inventing.

In the face of everything, Harry and Cecilia had brought this vision into being.

Eddie watched from the window and loved all his grandchildren again, especially Kevin, but was proudest of Harry, who had drawn them all to his driveway and kept them going—through the isolation of the pandemic, which even now was not done with them, no matter what people wanted to believe. Proud and devoted and so worn out with waiting, as old as he was and as violent as the disease at its extreme could be, he was willing at last to take whatever risk remained. Even Simone would join them once they got downtown. And Deirdre. How had he lived next door to this woman for so many years and never until now known her?

(Still in her kitchen, Deirdre finished packing bread into baskets. She had baked all day the day before and much of the night until crashing into sleep, and she had skipped the usual routine of the early hours of morning to get the last loaves out of the refrigerator and into the oven in time for departure. She was tired but energized, and happy that she would be riding with Eddie in his car. They would go slow, following the parade of musicians, children, actors, puppets—magicians that they all had become—until finally they would park and walk with the crowd. It would be a joyful crowd, despite the solemn reasons for its coming into being. The whole city would be there, a massive display of celebration and protest. How could it be anything but joyful? The lockdowns were all but over—again, for now—almost over; the last wildfire had been contained and smoke was thinning; the sun was bright, the air almost clear, and a lovely breeze was blowing; at all levels of government, the demand for police accountability was being raised, shouted in the streets and council chambers and assembly halls, sometimes even heard, even acted on, responded to. Until the next fire, the next killing, the next viral surge, and despite the ever compounding occasions for protest, despite the ongoing and inseparable crises in climate, racial injustice, and health, militarization and war, catastrophic extremes of poverty and wealth and the machinations of the powerful along with the weak, even as the more immediate emergencies were coming to a respite if not to an end, and despite the everlasting need to make impossible but necessary demands, to cry aloud together for help for the earth and all her creatures — despite all this, and because of it, this day would be a day of joy. *And all shall be well*, she thought, a*nd all manner of thing shall be well.*)

NEXT DOOR, AGNES waited in her driveway, delayed as the crowd of kids and musicians and marionettes and great puppets on poles began to make its way into the street. Even though they were not yet drumming or playing or singing or dancing, in their costumes and high spirits they already presented a lively parade, on their way to the march. By the time she arrived herself, she would be in costume too, though hers would not be celebratory. The kids had a long walk ahead of them, especially with those puppets and that palanquin-like construction, lightweight though it looked, and Agnes was relieved to see the old people, Eddie and the woman from the other side, loading his car with water bottles and covered baskets and drums.

When he glanced up and waved at her, for a moment she was afraid he was about to come over and chat or invite her to join them. Instead he held the passenger door for the woman — Eddie so tall and the woman so tiny — then went around to the other side.

At least the old people would not be walking today, Agnes thought. Smoke from the most recent fire still hung in the air. The young could handle it, the smoke and the distance, and if they got tired, at some point, except for the palanquin and those puppet heads, they could spread out and get the metro or a bus.

She wondered how she would feel if the demonstration led to confrontation, and wielding a taser or rubber baton she had to face these people through layers of helmet and shield. She wondered whether they would know her. Most likely, even up close, they wouldn't — wouldn't know her anywhere but here, waiting patiently in her driveway.

Invisibility had its uses.

She worried for them. For the violence coming, whether to this day's crowd or the next. For their future of fire and flood.

She sat watching until they had gone, all of them, Eddie and the old woman in his car following behind the stragglers at the rear, and waited a few minutes longer, staring at the vacancy left in the wake of their

Nathanael West Died Unknown

FAYE GREENER IN 1939 was young, seventeen and beautiful, cold and ingenuous both, but by the end of the 1960s, heartbreak and defeat had begun to dismantle her brittle glamour enough that some seed of a life more authentic had begun to sprout, to grow.

The night Bobby Kennedy was shot in the Ambassador Hotel, she was working as a cocktail waitress, tired from the long, overcrowded hours, and in some way desperate to get home. No one waited at home for her but the cat she had acquired some ten years before when her boyfriend of that era walked out on her for another woman, one younger and more beautiful, leaving the cat, his cat, behind. In a decade of solitude she had come to love him, an orange tabby she had renamed Dorothy in rebellion against his gender and his original designation, which had been Bud.

The night Bobby Kennedy was shot, instead of going home, she sat on a barstool, smoking and waiting her turn to be questioned by investigators about what if anything she had seen.

She was thinking with a little surprise that she ought to have been more shaken. She liked Bobby Kennedy. She didn't pay a lot of attention to politics but she liked that he seemed to care about ordinary people, little people, like herself. She liked that he seemed to be shy, but was handsome just the same. She liked that mop of hair, and his anger about manmade brutalities like war and poverty and the assassination of his brother. He wasn't showy or bombastic. You could feel his human heart.

SHE HAD BEEN around long enough. She knew a trick or two. But it didn't interest her anymore, if it ever had, to play by convenient or conventional rules. She had stopped trying. Still, she saw herself wanting to flirt with the officer who interviewed her. She wanted him to take her number, to check her out. She knew her face was tired, everything about her spent, the visible and the invisible both.

"Give me a call," she said before he let her go. "I don't know anything," she added, to make sure he understood the invitation was personal. She watched him blush. He was a boy, really, compared to her. "I'm sorry," she said. "Don't mind me. It's been a long night."

•

TOD, OF COURSE, had not been his name—the man who wrote about her when she was so young, the man who filled his stand-in character "Tod" with rape fantasies about her beautiful young self and never touched her, except that once, when he tried to kiss her and she pushed him away, or didn't, because who could really say anymore how far that kiss had gone, or would have? "Tod" was a made-up man, and the man himself, the writer, didn't really mean it, and that was the truth. He loved his wife. Or other men. Or himself. Everyone but her. She was just a vessel for his imagination, a vessel to fill with words, his own words, never hers.

She liked to think he had ruined her life, writing about her that way, making her conscious of herself. She had not asked for that, and maybe some intuition of what was coming accounted for her fear of him. She, who otherwise was fearless, yes, had been afraid of him. He was nothing like the big blond buffoonish Ivy League Tod he made himself out to be for the sake of his lying story. He had always made himself something he wasn't. Dark, wiry, clever, fast-talking or bitterly silent, all New York and jive. He had a power over her. She knew that. She didn't know why.

If he was nothing like his made-up Tod in his person, maybe in ambition, yes, he was. Megalomaniacal. Apocalyptic. Visionary, they would say after he died, after they re-discovered him, even though he had got everything wrong. Not right away when he died, because despite the books he died pretty much unknown. But what they said when he was alive didn't matter. It washed off him like the rain. What she said didn't matter, either. She was no one to him once his book was written. And once she read the book, he was no one to her. Once she saw herself there and not herself. Saw him and not him. Understood something she had never before that reading understood. After all those days and nights, those stolen moments, those phony ecstasies. Understood at last how young she was, had always been. She read the book—like everyone else, after he died, years after he died—and saw what she had taken for reality as the lie.

THE OFFICER DID phone her. His name was Josh. He liked her to call him by his last name. She could see it seemed to fortify him, made him feel older, stronger. She indulged him, or compromised by calling him Joshua, the name of a hero. "I'm forty-six years old, Joshua," she would say. As if to rub it in, the decade's difference in their ages. She didn't mean to be cruel. She didn't know what he saw in her. Or really what she saw in him. Just his desire, the adoration in his pale gray eyes. She could feel his hands touching her breasts, her soft flesh everywhere, when all he had done was glance at her in that way he had. It was enough. It was odd, she thought, she knew, that this simple truth—because it was a truth—could be enough.

"Joshua," she said, and he would come to her and enfold her. There was a simplicity to him. With him. She would be sorry when he left her, as she was certain he would. If not right away, then when she finally showed him the book. When she told him she was that girl, that cold ungiving selfish girl the artist hero was always wanting to rape.

The worst thing was when people talked about that book as if it was a love story: Tod loved the beautiful Faye, but she was shallow, ambitious, and calculating and wouldn't give him the sex he craved with her because in her heartless heart she loved him too. Or something like that. She hadn't read the thing in years. But whatever anyone said about it, it was all nonsense from her point of view.

Of course, her name wasn't actually Faye, or Greener, and never had been. That was the writer's doing. Her own name was Freya. If she had ever been shallow, ambitious, and calculating, that was pretty much over now, too. More likely—she thought this was true—those had been the writer's own characteristics, and she had contributed nothing more to his fantasy than her seventeen-year-old body as an object for his lust, along with her repeated refusals, which came from neither hidden motive nor cruelty. She had simply been a kid.

The writer, in fact, had been older than her father, by three years exactly—they shared a birthday. Like her father he had dropped out of high school, but unlike her father, who had educated himself by reading and roaming and living in the world, the writer had forged and stolen a history for himself and studied at Tufts and Brown before fleeing briefly to Paris and changing his name. He did get a kick out of her father, just like Tod with Harry, Faye's father in the book, that part was true. Or she had thought so back then. Her own father had been a magnetic man, intense and slender, a con artist in his own right, a kid himself when she was born. Her mother had not so much died as wandered off, but the effect on Freya was the same. She was a little girl alone with her daddy. The two men were much alike, in minor aspects too—slim, with dark eyes and stylish moustaches. But where the writer was homely and worked hard at his writing, her father was handsome and merely glib.

He brought home the bacon, as he liked to say, a reporter on the city beat at the *Examiner*, covering murders and cops and hookers and gambling. He loved their seedy world. It gave him an air, and Freya loved it with him, that world of actors and grifters and dime-store cowboys that the writer put into his book. And her father wasn't lost and pathetic like the made-up Harry Greener. Her father was a wicked playful little god.

That night in 1968 when she sat at the bar waiting to be talked to by the police, she had been thinking about her father, by then deceased. He would have loved this, she was thinking. Not the shooting—her father would have liked Bobby Kennedy, who would most likely soon be dead—but he would have reveled in the world Bobby's killing revealed. The chaos that was coming. The layers of lies.

She didn't think of her father often, anymore. Not since he'd died. Once a year on the anniversary of his death. And even that she sometimes forgot.

Later, living with Joshua would bring her father back, in odd moments. Something in his big gentle way with her. His devotion. The smell of his cigarettes, his stale sweat. The fact of him as a man. Joshua. Unlike her father in every other way. Even Dorothy seemed to love him, rubbed up against his stockinged feet, then suddenly attacked.

A UNIFORMED POLICEMAN had collected her from the bar and led her to the booth where Joshua sat taking statements from employees. He was a big man, his rolled-up white shirtsleeves exposing pale meaty forearms, reddish golden hairs, a nautical tattoo, and it was only when she seated herself and he looked up from his papers and met her eyes that she really saw him and felt again in that moment, as if she had forgotten, what pain they were in, what pain they all were in.

He introduced himself and took her name and details. He asked where she had been when the shots were fired, what she had heard and seen before and after, what she might have observed.

They had captured the gunman, hadn't they? Nothing she said, she thought, could have been of any use.

"I believe I'm a forgotten soul," she said to him that night they met, and he laughed and said, "Who could forget you?"

Maybe she should have known even then.

Waiting for her turn with him, she had also been thinking about the book, that false portrait of herself but also of the city—the packed-in crowds all evening and after the shock of the shooting calling up the writer's final vision, his hungry resentful mob gone mad, his city burning. But that man's apocalyptic fever, like his other fevers, got everything wrong. The city that night while Bobby was dying didn't rage, it grieved.

THIRTY YEARS LATER, Joshua was still with her when he retired. She was older than he was, but they were aging well together. She had never had children, but he had two from his first marriage, and they shared his grandchildren, who called her Auntie Freya. Dorothy was long gone, replaced by a pair of Siamese, Uno and Dos. Joshua's idea, indulging one of the grandkids. Whatever. Retirement didn't suit him. They tried going on a cruise. The cruise didn't suit him either. Everything made him restless. Herself, she was always at peace. He came to her for comfort, day after day, year after year, until she woke up one morning and discovered she had survived him.

Now she was alone. Except for her neighbors in the care home and the aides and nurses, mostly alone. She sat in her rocking chair and watched movies she couldn't hear. She knew them by heart, she'd seen them so often, over so many years. They were like birds to her, or butterflies at the window. They were flowers, arrays of color and motion and light. So many of the people she saw on the screen had died during her lifetime. Sometimes she saw this in the images. Sometimes she remembered.

The fiftieth anniversary of Bobby's assassination brought everything back, and from then on, year after year. That night at the Ambassador with Joshua when they met. His eyes caressing her. How alive he was and made her feel. How up until that moment, she had not felt alive since reading the writer's treatment of her: her desires mocked, her youth and beauty tarnished, her dreams cast into mud.

Contempt had been his weapon. His belief in his own genius. His vast unique enlightenment. He craved followers, recognition, devotion. (The writer? Maybe her father. She sometimes got the two confused.) It should have given her satisfaction, just a little, she thought, that he hadn't lived to see his own fame. But his fame only made his portrait of her worse. He had drawn her stupid and malicious, innocent and conniving. He had stolen her from herself entirely. He had crushed whatever trust in another human being she might have been able to achieve.

Until suddenly, with Joshua, the writer was erased, as if erased.

And yet, in forty years together, even though she had told him

BIANCA IS IN Arizona visiting her mother when she admits to herself that she's pregnant. Probably. She knows how pregnant feels. She was pregnant once before and as a consequence lives with a beautiful six-year-old daughter and across town from the good ex-husband. Now she also has an ex-lover, or moocher, or whatever he was, but definitely, definitively ex-, and she does not want him back in her life in any way, having finally, with significant effort, got rid of him. That she might now be pregnant with what will be his child if she gives birth to it makes her skin crawl.

She's sitting up late, watching a movie on her mother's old-fashioned television (her mother, who refuses to get cable or flat screen, let alone wi-fi and Netflix). Bianca can't figure out what world her mother lives in, or when she became so backward and resistant to change. Lucy — her mother — is barely sixty years old. In her own real life (Bianca does not think of her mother's house in Arizona as real life) she knows people a decade older and more who live active lives online.

The movie isn't good and she's only half watching, but she sits up with it just the same, savoring the time alone and drinking from her mother's rarely touched stash.

NOIR. IMAGES IN black and white, with heavy shadows, fog and cigarette smoke.

There's a man, of course, whose face we can't see. Only his hat, his overcoat, his hand. We're back in the day when even in Los Angeles men wear overcoats and fedoras.

There's a woman, too. We can't see her either, just a silvery fall of long wavy apparently golden hair.

A shadow on the carpet. A pool of blood. A body? Maybe. Maybe a man, a white shirt. He might as well be naked. In those days a white shirt could indicate nakedness — the intimacy of being at home, or as if at home, at home in someone else's — the way being in bed wearing a bra or bare-chested with boxers can indicate nakedness now. The music is ominous.

Cut.

An iron. Resting upright on an ironing board. A kitchen window, morning sunlight, birds outside. Child on a swing. A woman, wearing an apron, cooking an egg. A pair of scissors on the table, an article or advertisement clipped from a newspaper. Close up: an obituary. The woman is blithe, her hair dark and bobbed. No sign anywhere of the cascading white waves that signified the blonde. The child, a boy in a striped T-shirt, runs inside, and in the impossibly chipper voice of movie children of that era asks for toast and when will Daddy be home.

"If there were no politics," a man's voice says, as the image dissolves to an overflowing ashtray, a desk piled chaotically with papers, rising on another white shirt, unbuttoned at the collar, worn with suspenders, sleeves rolled up to the elbow, the man at the desk smoking a cigarette and talking into a black telephone (yes, that's a phone). Dark slicked-back hair and a mustache. A handsome face, a cynical edge to his words, laughter under the snarl and smile.

WHEN A COMMERCIAL comes on, Bianca hits the mute button—at least her mother has a remote—and gets up to refresh her drink.

She does not want to be pregnant. She does not plan to be pregnant. One child is enough for her. One daughter. Stella, only six years old, already breaks her heart, and Bianca has no room for a second Cody. She senses the germinating seed would make itself a boy, but whatever the gender, it will be half its father if she allows it to continue to grow. She knows it as an evil, on the thought of it alone. A dead thing, cold, reptilian, trying to take hold of her, to swallow her up, just like the man who planted it there, believing he could compete with Stella for her love.

She sits down with her drink and unmutes the movie as the newspaperman who looks so much like her father walks without an umbrella through darkness and rain to wait under a streetlamp for a stranger.

But as soon as the encounter begins, Lucy, her mother, is up from bed and in the living room, coming to sit with her, wanting to talk, wanting Bianca to talk, begging her to talk and most of all to say, "I love you."

"I love you," her mother says. Not for the first time. "Talk to me."

And Bianca wants to scream.

IN TRUE NOIR we would enter a plot, investigate the body, encounter a dangerous but beautiful woman, seen through the eyes of the hard-bitten detective or reporter, seduced or not but always compelled, drawn into whatever darkness produced the corpse, which is never a deeper darkness than the detective's or reporter's own, as, incident after incident, he survives, and we along with him.

But this is not true noir. This is a childhood in its shadow, in its shape, inflected, dramatized. A childhood made of illusion.

This child is not a boy, but a girl. There is no iron in the kitchen, no swing set in the yard. The mother does not wear a ruffled apron and does not cook an egg, and generations later, the man behind the desk with cigarette and phone is turning pancakes on a griddle, standing at the stove.

The little girl loves her daddy, and even when she grows up, when she is, briefly, married, when she has her own kitchen and her own little girl, Daddy will still be the one she loves.

He was an outlaw himself, an aspiring bad guy, later recovering, but never not an outlaw until the day he prematurely died.

Noir comes in variants, of course—sometimes our guiding character is not a detective or reporter, sometimes the body comes later, sometimes he doesn't survive, or she—and even so, what is fundamental persists: a world of power, a system of relationships, only indirectly implicated, unnameable and out of reach—the named and reachable by definition already sacrificed, cut loose.

CODY HAD LONG legs and sad blue eyes and when Bianca first met him skinny hips. He wore his dark hair tied at the back of his neck in an old-fashioned ponytail, curly wisps floating at his ears. He was beautiful then, and for a longish time she knew him as Stella's babysitter's boyfriend, until he and the babysitter broke up. Something started to happen between them after that, not right away. By the time they met again, Stella was in daycare and school, and Cody was beefier, as if the skinny hips had been an illusion, or a trick of memory. It turned out he was bulking up on purpose, building muscle that would one day turn to flab she figures now. He was like that, she wants to think—in with a bang, out with a whimper. The ponytail was gone, replaced by a trendy bad-boy undercut. He had no idea who he was, just opinions and a style received from his latest girlfriend, a woman who was keeping him, more or less. He didn't work, just worked out, he told Bianca. He was cheating on that woman even to have a drink with her, let alone when she took him home, when he fucked her and with a fake show of hesitation stayed the night.

Bianca was under his spell for months—not many months, maybe three, maybe four. Or maybe longer. She doesn't like to think about it, even to count. She's been happy to be rid of him. He used to tell her she lived too much in her head. "Well, yeah," she'd say back at him, "I've got voices there to listen to and they're way more interesting than you." Or words to that effect. But that was after the trouble started. There had been a time before.

First the joy, then the nitpicking, then the fighting over Stella, until she exiled him to an inflatable mattress in the hall and told him to find himself another place to crash. He camped there for a month, saying he had nowhere to go, until the morning two weeks ago when she came back from taking Stella to school and yelled bloody murder at him—still naked on the air mattress, smirking up at her, lounging in her freshly laundered sheets. She gave him till she got home from work to move himself out, and his shit, and finally that night he was gone.

He had been a slow burn. The cult of Cody, she likes to think. One devotee at a time. Originally it was the babysitter, when Stella was two. Who knows who after that, then the rich woman, if she really was rich, or existed at all—how is she supposed to believe anything he ever told her? Then herself. Stella was a complication for him, though. He couldn't stand that Stella came first. "I gave up that woman," he said, more than once. "I left a rich woman who wanted to marry me, I left her for you, who had nothing to give me, but—"

"A place to live," Bianca would interject. "Free food."

Now she has to face the fact that he hasn't let her evict him so easily.

Unlike Stella, this new possible child would be a torment. A demon and nothing more. All Cody. Alien inside her body. An aberration. A violence. No part of herself.

That she's pregnant she considers to be entirely Cody's fault.

And meanwhile here was her mother, begging for her love.

On the screen the blonde sits at a bar, blowing cigarette smoke and showing off her hair.

Bianca has muted the sound but can't keep her eyes off the picture.

"Something's bothering you," Lucy's just said. "I know something's wrong. If you don't want to tell me, fine. But don't pretend everything is all right. Don't pretend you care about this stupid movie."

"The only thing bothering me," Bianca says, still watching the woman in the bar, the ice in her drink, the cigarette in her hand, her great mascaraed eyes, "is you insisting I say words that don't mean anything to me—" wondering how her mother can read her mood so accurately and still have no clue who she is or what she needs.

She adds, finally turning to look at her, "Not when they're coerced like this," hoping to soften without giving in. "I'm here, aren't I?"

"Are you?" Lucy asks, slamming up from the couch, then towering, immobile, glaring, helpless and raging both.

"Don't start," Bianca says, aware of the precipice, the potential for shouting, wailing, Stella waking up to ask what's going on. "Please, Mom," she says, as quiet and small as she can make herself, holding out a hand, an offering, to draw her mother back from the brink.

STELLA WAS THE best of her, Bianca thinks, and of Jason, and from the beginning her own complete little person.

They had chosen together not to be told the baby's sex before the birth. A boy would get Jason's father's name, a family tradition, just one of the many ways he and Bianca were nothing alike. She came from a family with no traditions to speak of. Together they decided on "Stella" for a girl, long before she arrived, because they understood her as coming to them from beyond the earth, their own universe. A gift. Unplanned and liberating. Even though they had chosen not to be told, Bianca had known in her heart from the beginning, long before she could feel her alive inside and kicking, that their baby would be a girl—until, almost suddenly, here she was, a night of labor and finally, as if all at once, a five-pound-thirteen-ounce bundle in her arms, at her breast, three weeks earlier than expected and complete in every part, their perfect Stella, their tiny star.

She and Jason would not have married without her, without the coming of her. Bianca had intended never to marry, never to be anyone's wife. She grew up with visions of a life all her own. Vague visions, sometimes coming into focus—working in video, working in clay, dance, set design, landscaping, horticulture, botany, astronomy, astrobiology, Russian literature, galactic exploration, and so on, one enthusiasm reshaping itself into another. She was good at languages but took that nowhere. Then she was in bed with Jason and she was pregnant, they loved each other, and it was easy to get married. But visions kept calling to her. Most of all she wanted to go back to school, wanted to study even though she didn't know yet what.

Jason supported her in all of it, her fluidity, her restlessness. She couldn't have said how it was that they separated, divorced. She sometimes wishes it had been something obvious, violation, a lover, a life of lies. But it had been nothing at all.

She found the babysitter, the office job, the oddly spacious one-bedroom apartment, moved with Stella almost to Pasadena, and started taking classes at night.

She's a disappointment to her mother, she knows, first for the marriage, then for the separation and divorce. Even more, for her failure to settle, to choose, to devote herself to a stable life, whether to one man or to one of her several gifts. Most of all, for her refusal to devote herself as a daughter, her refusal at twenty-six to walk in her mother's footsteps, to share her mother's tastes and politics and dreams, to embrace her gurus and cures—to embrace her mother at all, other than perfunctorily, her refusal even to repeat back to her a hollow declaration of love.

"IT'S NOT THAT I don't love you," she says, when Lucy sits again. "I just can't believe in the words. Not even with Stella. Of course, I love her. Of course, I do. And you. Whatever that means. But to say it—me here, you there—*I love you?* No, I can't do that. I can't honestly do that."

By now, Lucy is crying, but quietly, hazard bypassed, the strait between wrath and pain safely traversed.

She wants to go to Sedona in the morning, wants to take them, she says between sniffles, "You and Stella." Before she got up she was lying awake planning an excursion. Red rock and vortices. Crystals and UFOs. The City of the Star People. "An excursion will do us good," she says. "A day outdoors, fresh air and spirit energy. Maybe you'll see what I see. Living here."

"Come on, Mom," Bianca says, putting an arm around her, and, drawing her into a sideways hug, tries to reconcile the difference between the vastness of her mother's power over her and the hunger of the little bird body pressing awkwardly against hers on the couch.

They sit like this as long as Bianca can stand it, until finally she says, "Let's call it a night now. Go on back to bed."

She has to acquiesce to Sedona before Lucy will move.

Once she's gone, on the television, the volume still muted, Bianca sees an alleyway at night, crates piled high, a stray cat, a sewer grate billowing steam, shards of silver lamplight from the distant street, and a shadow—man, hand, gun.

She's lost whatever thread of the movie she had been following.

She knows it isn't fair exactly to blame Cody for her pregnancy.

She knows exactly how to blame herself.

"YOU'RE UNUSUALLY COMBATIVE," a therapist said to her once, the only time she's ever made an effort to see a therapist, shortly before she dropped out of school. "Do you know why?"

"Isn't that your job," Bianca shot back, "to figure that out?" and the therapy went nowhere. Five free sessions provided by the college and this the only moment she remembers.

"You never even took the sweater out of the box," her mother said. The soft fuzzy Easter-chick-yellow angora cardigan sent from her desert suburb for Christmas or a birthday not long after she left L.A. A color and style Bianca hasn't worn since she was six years old herself.

What was her mother even doing going through the shelves in Stella's closet?

"I don't dress like that," Bianca cried in despair and accusation. "I haven't dressed like that in twenty years."

What was the point?

SHE WATCHES THE film as if it's meant to be silent, imagining music and words. The character who resembles her father boards a train, looking back and forth over one shoulder, then the other, in an exaggerated gesture of being followed, chased. Bianca can almost hear the tension-heightening music. The blonde is on the train—quick glances of recognition, eyes cast down as if the two are strangers—and for a moment Bianca is curious to know what she's missed and almost unmutes the sound. The scene changes, just in time. Night is falling on a highway, headlights cutting through fog.

What killed her father was not this kind of noirish plot, but the sudden failure of his heart, apparently, and loss of control of the car he was driving at not quite breakneck speed. He had never taken care of himself. He had not lived well, or lived too well, depending on how you looked at it. He had failed at all his ambitions and he had not found rest or peace or ease. He drank a long time. If his heart hadn't given out, some other essential organ would have. Perhaps not accompanied by crash and burn. Alive, he had brought a radiance into any room he entered. Men and women loved him, and he basked in all that love, drank it up and relied on it to nourish his one precious life.

There was a cost to that, of course, a shadow, and he had no stand-in, no stunt double. He was on his own to pay the price. And those he left behind.

When he died, Lucy had behaved as if her life was over, for a year, two, three without him. Then found herself reborn. Left Los Angeles for the high desert. Left on a train. Just like the blonde in the movie. Now she comes back to the city to visit from time to time, sleeps on the air mattress in Bianca's hall, and searches her cupboards for evidence, an object to get hold of, to latch grievance onto, an occasion for complaint.

At the commercial, Bianca goes outside to smoke and look at the stars. One of the few good things about her mother's choice of a home—the dark sky, the brilliant night. The sky and moon and stars together offer respite and most nights here leave her wordless and free of distress. To-night, though, she can almost not see them, the smear of the galaxy, the dense pinpricks of light. *Twinkle twinkle little . . .* she thinks, and, how *I wonder . . .* She needs patience, time for her eyes to find themselves in the darkness. She sits and watches and listens—shrieks, trills, warbles, long extended howls, rat-a-tat-tats as if on a drum—the night sounds so near, so now, each creature its own voice, and no knowing what creature it is, what language, what need it cries out of.

The stars' light comes from the past, she thinks, and then, like one of her mother's believers in crazy—but what if it comes from the future too?

She tosses what's left of her cigarette, watching it spark across the darkness.

If she continues with school long enough, maybe she'll understand her own question, what makes it sense or nonsense, or both. Maybe she'll learn to recognize these creatures that animate the night. For now, she'd settle with knowing how she got herself into this mess with Cody. How she had wanted him so intensely and hated him so absolutely and let him stay around so much longer than she meant to. How she had let him get his evil hooks into her—which is how the whole thing feels to her now. Hooked. Evil. When she had begged for those hooks, begged him to stay, to move in, to make love to her, to give up the other woman.

Who—what but a demon—could have chosen their wrathful cou-pling as a call to incarnation?

·

THE PREGNANCY MUST have begun, she thinks, the night before she moved him out of her bed. She was already leaving him, almost knew she was leaving, but craved another night of sex, knew she was pushing the calendar, just on the edge of fertility, not using the diaphragm and gel, but took the chance. It was worth it, she thought at the time—after rage, hunger, and frenzy, all soft and broken open. Then in the morning he was on her as usual about smoking and ignoring him for Stella—getting their breakfast, talking nonsense with her, brushing her hair, the ordinary start of a day—and Bianca shut him down. Before leaving with Stella for school and work, she dragged the air mattress out of the closet and told Cody to inflate it, to move himself into the alcove, and then to start looking for another place to live.

He reacted as if she was joking, smirked, humoring her, pretended to do as she asked, collected his few books and clothes and settled himself into the hall, confident she would change her mind, as time went on meeting her with looks of distant amusement and mild disdain. They lived like that in silence for a month until finally she exploded.

Now that he's gone, though, she has to admit that he had been right about a few things. The smoker's phlegm she coughs up and leaves in the bathroom sink every morning. Yes, it was—it *is* gross. Yes, she should wash it away. She does here, for Lucy, just not for herself, and not for Stella, and didn't for him. And, yes, she should quit smoking. Yes, maybe he was even right about the bedroom, that it should have been theirs instead of Stella's. If she had loved him enough. Or whatever. But the more he complained of her coughing and tried to make her quit, the more smoking she did; the more he complained that Stella was overindulged, the more indulgence Bianca gave her; and the more he complained about her choices in birth control, the riskier she got.

Birth control was at the heart of their problem. Or crystallized the problem between them. She wouldn't take pills. She had stopped when she left Jason, didn't intend to have a regular partner and hated the way being on the pill every day made her feel, more vulnerable and volatile than without. Instead, she kept track of her fertility cycle and when necessary inserted diaphragm and spermicide. Cody couldn't stand it, refused to make love to her, said knowing there was poison inside her waiting to kill his sperm turned him off—Cody who was obsessed with overpopulation and vowed repeatedly never to have children. He wanted her back on the pill or fitted for an IUD. He wouldn't use a condom, insisted he was clean and trusted she was. She might have gone for the IUD, eventually. But the more he pushed, the more she resisted. And apparently, after all, he had been right about that too.

The one thing, though, that she will never allow him to have been right about is her devotion to Stella. Stella would always come first.

THE DARKNESS OF the film, forgotten, fills the stillness of the night, and she would like to sit out in this darkness and stillness for hours—as if caged in a telescope, the vast night all to herself, solitary observer in a world without distinction between demand and request, no difference that matters, in a place of pure aspiration, *ad astra*, no constellations of karmic habit and recurring disaster, no bad stars, no possibility of opposing the stars or being opposed by them, nothing personal, no parents and children, no disappointments and expectations, no lives to be interrupted or taken or broken or stopped or lost. She would like the darkness to deepen, to clarify, the stars to show themselves, undiminished, each in its luminosity. She would like the night to burst open, the stars to flare, young giants to reveal their coronae to her naked eye.

Tomorrow she and Lucy and Stella will drive and walk in the desert and saturate their senses with blues and greens and reds, with sun, sky, scrub, trees, cliffs, rock. They'll walk through a cradle that demands silence, but Stella will talk and Lucy will talk, and aware that her own silence would hurt the one and anger the other, Bianca will chatter along with them. And what will be the point?

If you're not a demon, she says in silence to the nascent creature, *if you're just on the way to being an ordinary little human, I'm sorry. If you came to us and chose us for your parents, I'm sorry. If you wanted Stella for your sister or Lucy for your grandma, I don't know. I don't know what I'm taking from you. You're not visible to me. But Stella is. And I am. And for us, I have to say no. I have to say no to you. Find a better mother. A better father. A happier possible life. May it be a blessing to you to be erased so early in this journey. Maybe you even get points for that, who knows? Go back to the stars and try again.*

THE MAN ON the train is going to die. Bianca can see that. The blonde will escape. She has the money, whatever money it is, whatever it was she conned him into doing to get it for her. For them, she led him to think. She had him in a double bind. Or something like that. She is the victor. The train chugs along through the night as almost slowly the body falls away, out the gap between cars, his body, his stand-in, or stunt double, the actor who looked so much like Bianca's father. Gone.

She turns off the television, the movie over. In the morning she'll ask Stella what she wants to do. Go for a ride with Grandma to see the red rocks and bathe in the hot springs? Visit the observatory, its telescopes, the Omniglobe? Or drive back across the desert, two days early, home to the city, straight through and fast, like fugitives, or rest the night in Joshua Tree and sleep out under the stars?

She will stop and buy a pregnancy test as soon as they've left her mother.

The test will confirm what her body already knows.

For that day or two, on the way home, she will allow the possibility, the potential alive inside her, Stella's little brother or sister, unfolding, unrevealed. But not for any longer. She will schedule the appointment while she and Stella are still on the road. She will call and ask Jason to accompany her on the day of the procedure. Jason will hold the silence and darkness with her. Stella will go to school and daycare as usual, and no one, not Cody, not Lucy, not anyone, will ever after have to be told.

Invisible Woman Dancing in a Cage

MARVELING AT THE sensation of grit beneath her cheek. Marveling at the silence. Nearby, people huddle or lie flat out on the ground. Others, upright or crouching, stumble or run, around or across her, in bursts—feet, sandals, boots. So much sporadic motion and Trinity hears nothing. She did not so much fall as drop reflexively. She feels no injury, no pain. The last image, the butterfly girl's face splattered red. The image now, her own left hand at rest beside her eyes and beyond it the garland of wilting flowers and ribbons given to her by strangers early in the day. She wriggles her fingers and taps the slate beneath her, reaches for an orange streamer, the crushed daisies and lilies, pushes with her other hand to inch herself forward, wants to rescue it, her crown, to protect it from the mindless runners and their feet.

Whatever happened must still be going on. And still in silence.

Unsettling to see so clearly and hear nothing. A buzzing maybe, a hum. Like wax or cotton in her ears. And her sight so bright, everything haloed, rimmed with a tiny band of light. Sparkling. A day made of diamonds.

HER COAT, SO thin, in the early morning had been insufficient. She had wanted the sun to come out, to reach her, remembering from childhood that story of Sun and Wind competing to prove which was the stronger by success in stripping some poor traveler of his cloak. Wind blew hard and harder to whip the cloak away; then Sun bore down in all his heat and glory. You know who won. A metaphor for love, for persuasion. No one ever talked about the sun's guile in proposing the contest in the first place, or the wind's folly in accepting. (Was this metaphor too?) She could use a little love and persuasion herself, she thought, duplicitous or not, even though, indifferent to warmth and cold, she would wear her threadbare coat even in the heat of day.

Now and then, people walked past her—some with coats, some without. Observing what they wore was how she read the weather. She had no immediate sense of the weather herself anymore—what was the point? She lived out in it, outside, except when powers-that-be forced her into shelter.

Shelter, she thought. Words had lost their meaning. Just in her life-time, which the older she got the shorter she understood it to be.

Still, sometimes she wished for a better coat, one big enough and thick enough to hide in, to disappear inside of, the kind of coat you would take off in the heat of the sun, even she, who never took anything off, not on the street—big and downy soft, a bed of a coat, a shelter all its own, a pillow, a mattress, a world, a whole world in a coat, a coat with pockets where she would keep her treasures—the necklace of wooden beads she wore wrapped around her wrist, the chocolate bar a child had given her so precious she would never eat it, the chartreuse strap with the key to her mother's house, the house that was no longer her mother's, or hers anymore either, the photo in a tiny plastic or more likely ivory frame of her mother's ancient grandma—

A coat like that would be a treasure in itself, and Trinity bent her mind trying to fold that coat into its pockets.

SLEEPWALKING IN THE early morning, she had left the camp for a prettier, quieter spot. More cars, but fewer people, nobody making a home on the sidewalk. She was quiet herself, immobile, planted, even when another person hurried past, but the quieter her body, the faster her mind. *In jail the girls used to say we were the witches.* Now she thinks maybe they're the androids—*they, we, all of us.* She keeps up with the news. On television screens in public places she had watched the faces of candidates for of-fice and winners and losers. There had been a wooden handsome man, a white man with blue eyes and a granite jaw, and watching him she had heard herself saying out loud that white men with blue eyes and granite jaws had no credibility anymore, adding without saying aloud, *if they ever did have.*

Memory blurred. There was a man like that, more than one, some-where in her past.

But her past was long.

She had first known sex in her sleep.

Keeping up with things in that world she no longer lived in, she caught details that still surprised her. It was strange to be surprised, as old as she was. She was shocked when she learned that a husband or lover entering a woman during sleep was regarded now as violation—shocked, and maybe ashamed. To be entered like that had been among her own unspoken desires—to wake with a man she wanted moving inside her, to wake into her body's coming.

Not all surprise was unpleasant.

She had been enchanted when she heard about an 11th-century indigenous city, long buried and dead, across the Mississippi from what had become St. Louis by the time her mother's very young future grandma landed there from Ireland; and, even as her own friends on the street sickened from the virus, she had been for an instant delighted on seeing it reported that the killer got its name from protein spikes radiating outward like points of a crown, the halo of a star.

But shock was more potent than surprise.

Like that, unknowing, she had lost her virginity, the virginity she had been trying so hard to lose — drunk and fumbling with the boy, giving up and passing out together on his friend's couch, then waking with a great humming of her body just as the friend walked in and the boy stopped working. "Too bad," he said, pulling out, "we were going pretty good there," and never entered her again.

When later other boys followed, and men, she wanted this thing repeated, to be taken by surprise by whatever man she gave herself to, or desired or loved, wanted him to get to her under the radar like that, her busy mind shut off, the noise of her thinking, wanted to awaken into that wordless buzzing body. And now they said this desire was abnormal, perverse? A mark of trauma? A sign of surrender to patriarchal entitlement? An abandonment of agency? (What agency?) Was she supposed to believe this?

Even the question made her want to laugh.

Still, whenever she saw one of those headlines, or one of those #MeToo faces on a screen, the question came back to assail her.

She knew it was too late to care now, that part of her life long over, and knew too that her craving for entry in unconsciousness, not as violation but surrender, beyond surrender, had started long before the drunk and fumbling boy, when she was too young to know desire for what it was, or entitlement, or patriarchy, but knew even then, already, this mind that goes on and on.

NEAR THE CORNER where she was sitting — on a concrete ledge that ran alongside a building and invited her to sit as she almost passed it by — *no, not literally, be careful how you express yourself, even in your thoughts, no knowing who can hear them* — near this corner there was a strip of garden, a concrete planter big enough for weeds and wild grasses along with poppies and snapdragons and dianthus and lobelia and a giant sunflower rising overhead. It was a perfect spot to sit, to watch the living flowers there, the birds that came and landed or flew off, now and then a butterfly, and after watching long enough, bees and spiders and even ants.

The spiders reminded her of her childhood, how she had loved to watch them, out in the backyard of the house she had lost—one in particular, gold and black, striped like a tiger, perched at the center of a big web that glittered with morning dew. She had been an only child, but there had come after her a brother and a sister, unborn, dead born, an absence abiding throughout her life. She was a trinity. She told people this was her name. When they signed her into a shelter, "Trinity," she said.

It wasn't the name on her ID.

"Maybe not," she said. "But it's what I go by."

The name on her ID was who she had been when she lost her mother's house.

She wasn't meant to lose the house, but then she was never meant to have a house in the first place—her mother and father either. Who were their people anyway? Who did they think they were? It was all she could do to bury her mother, let alone what it took to keep up with a mortgage.

None of this would have been obvious to them, to her mother or her father, to his many brothers, not during their lifetimes, or even now, so late, when her own life was approaching its end.

Even now, if they were still here, alive, she thought, she knew, they would not be able to see it.

BUT WHAT *IT*? she wondered, lost to whatever thought had come just before.

The sun was higher now, shining, its heat almost reaching her. The people passing her by had changed. No longer scurrying, they came in clusters, more of them, more frequently, and they milled. There had been a lull, an emptiness, then new groupings, with music and costumes and drums and home-painted signs saying things like ACT NOW, BLACK LIVES MATTER, CLIMATE JUSTICE IS RACIAL JUSTICE, THERE IS NO PLANET B.

She preferred seeing the pictures on the signs to reading the words—the green and blue planet, silhouettes of oil rigs and a processing plant against an orange sunset, dollar signs shaped into rainbows, photographs of animals lost, and in the street with the costumed people, puppets made to look like wildcats and wolves.

In the crowd, among the dancers, suddenly, impossibly, she caught a glimpse of Araceli—Araceli who had long ago been her roommate in a city up north, teaching Spanish part-time and writing poetry that she sent home to a small press in Veracruz. That girl in the street wearing butterflies and palm trees—butterflies masking her face, bright diaphanous wings sweeping out behind her, palm fronds flying up with her arms and unfurling with her skirt, her hair, long and black and thick with the same snaking curls—that girl was not, of course, Araceli, but had brought Araceli to mind, Araceli who had wanted to love her, Trinity, in all her three-ness, when they were both so young, the Araceli that Trinity had wanted to love, not as she loved men, but as she loved the unborn sister she both was and wasn't, as she would have loved a child that was and wasn't herself, Araceli who read for her aloud in Spanish her newborn poems, Spanish a language Trinity only patchily understood, while together they drank, and danced, and wept for all that was and wasn't their life.

"I CAN'T TELL you how I've longed for this town," she had said, or something like that, to a friend she hadn't seen in all the years she'd been away, or any time since, words alive in her mind now, as if she were still far from home. "The way it was," she said, or the words went—something about the way it was slow then, the way at night you could drive and drive fast into darkness and head- and taillights under freeway signs lit up green in the sky, or were they blue?—everything else invisible, just the motion and roar and the balmy night, going nowhere, the beach maybe, or the airport, or all the way to Mexico, speed and silence, or music, what was that radio station? All those old pop forty songs?

"A hunger came over me for that," she said to her friend, the smell of the water and sand, the feel of the air, the indigo sky over the ocean, or glowing red over the rooftops toward downtown, planes replacing the stars and sweeping klieg lights erasing them. "We used to go to the airport and stand on the roof and watch the planes take off and rise up right over our heads." She had wanted that again, wanted the life of easy weather, rain and fog and sun, the sky always radiant, the darkness soothing on the skin. She made it worse for herself, dwelling on it. It was never like that, and even when it was, she had been full of longing then too, the longing to get away, the constant desire to leave, to be on one of those planes or across the border, to live in a bigger world.

"Even now," she had said to that friend when she first came back, "I'm missing the city right here, so changed, so many lifetimes later, walking with you, the joy in being able to walk, the way we did when we were kids, allowed to go a few blocks alone across La Tijera to the liquor store, clutching our nickels for candy, or down into the gully they buried with the San Diego Freeway, now the 405. I'm happy not to be driving, if only for this hour. But this hour, enjoying it just as it is, doesn't relieve the longing for the way it used to be, for the scrubby little laurels and dirty eucalyptus, the falling down palms. I want what I want. I want to be sixteen again. I want to be sitting in a car outside my father's house with a boy who's afraid to touch me, listening to Barry-whoever-it-was rage on the eve of destruction and Mick Jagger try and try and get none. I want to be that girl again. Before that world came to an end."

A WAVE OF people draped in red oozed through the street in front of her—oozed because of how they moved, in slow motion and silent, en-acting loss and sorrow, their faces painted white, their eyes black-rimmed and dripping black-painted tears above the black or white masks that covered their mouths and noses. Across the street, on the other side of the scarlet dancers, half a dozen uniformed police stood watching, and Trinity caught one of them studying her, a man, young and Black, his whole body a question. She could count the seconds until he would part the crowd and cross the street to come and ask what she was doing, did she need help, did she have a place to stay—she wasn't begging here, was she?—ready to write her up.

She wondered what he saw when he saw her, an old white lady in shabby clothes. Not carrying anything, no telltale shopping cart, no plas-tic bag. Her face rugged but clean, if not her hair. She could be any old white lady, resting her bones. She even wore a clean blue paper surgical mask, still following all the rules.

"Trinity," she answered, when he finally stood above her, taller than she'd expected from across the street, and younger. "Just sitting enjoying the sun." Trying to show him an emotionless response.

"This license is expired," he said.

"And me with nothing to drive."

"Time to move on, Miss Trinity," he said, gently, as if she were his own old auntie.

"You want me to join that crowd?" she asked, the silent dancers having passed and the crowd just then getting rowdier, denser, parade and street festival and protest all rolling into one.

"Whatever," he said. He didn't like her tone, she could tell. "You can't just sit here all day."

"I think I can," she said and flinched. She didn't mean to pitch him a tone.

"You want to try it?"

She met him steadily in the eye and saw he would not back down. She had been too cocky with him, too entitled, too white. She still didn't know how to shed these things, after so many years. For a long time in her life, without her consent or even her knowing, their existence had protected her. But everything changed on the street.

(For a time, when the virus was new, nurses and social workers had come around trying to get her and her people to leave the camp — *no way, right?* — but they'd also brought in extra toilets and handwashing stations and for a while she was able to keep herself clean — not her clothes only, but parts of her body too — without having to spend a night in a hotel just to get a decent shower. She never slept well inside anymore and she watched too much bad TV. She had a little money. Deposited every month. She still had a bank account. Cash to spend on laundry, food. Money that paid for the storage unit she visited twice a year. It all just happened automatically, the dollars went in, the dollars went out. She drew from an ATM. She wore her card around her neck, clipped to the chartreuse lanyard with her expired driver's license and her mother's key, under her clothes, next to her skin. She'd worked most of her life, after all. Not doing much, but the hours added up. She just didn't have a house anymore, a shelter to live inside of, not for years. For a while, at first, when she lost the house, she had stayed with friends, a few months here, a few months there. But there hadn't been enough friends in the city to sustain that as a life. She told herself in those first months that she should leave, find a city or town that she could afford. But she didn't want to go. Never again. One of those old friends still let her use his address, and an address was all she needed now from anyone she had known before. She even voted from that address of his — *thank you, Jesus*. She had enough, more than enough, so much that she sometimes gave money away. She had people to take care of, her own new people to sustain.)

By the time she mumbled an apology to the policeman and readied herself to push up from the ledge, a few youngsters from the crowd had stopped to watch, from a small distance, preparing to witness, bringing out their phones. She apologized again to the man, and as she launched herself, he reached for her elbow to help.

Pretending to hesitate in search of balance and shrugging him off, she exaggerated a shuffle, a hunch, wanting to shame him a little, while the young people who had been watching drew her into their circle, one offering an orange to eat, another a garland of flowers braided with bright colored ribbons for streamers, then placed it on her head.

After that she marched along with them. It was a happy circle to be part of, young people all around her, painted and costumed and clean, singing and chanting and playing their drums.

SOME OF HER friends from the street had fallen sick from the virus and some had moved indoors to emergency shelters and three had died. At first, they had all been cavalier. They called it a rich person's disease. *Who goes on a cruise, yeah? Who flies to Italy?* But then it came home. No one wanted to leave the street, inside it could only be worse. When the city set up new beds in rec centers and moved the oldest and sickest into them, Trinity and her neighbors were policed to keep their tents at a distance to one another, to slow the contagion. Some of the young ones went back to their mothers. Best thing for them, and Trinity helped some of them go, bought them bus fare or whatever they needed. She missed them, but that's how it was. And the virus wasn't over. If not this plague, then the next. Life was precarious, nothing new. Everybody had a story.

The city had been so quiet then, at first, during the virus. She had still gone out every day to walk and to find a place to sit. When an officer tried to stop her she had argued with him and won—why should it be only householding people who were allowed to go for a walk? It wasn't as if she was going to get up close and personal with anyone. She sat herself down in the sun, anywhere with flowers, and talked to her brother and sister and listened for them to speak. They spoke to her more easily in the quiet. All in all a peaceful time.

When the first of her people died, she had masked up and taken the bus out to the mostly empty beach and spent a few days there, sitting on a bench or lying in sand or staring at the Ferris wheel, imagining it still going up and around and down. Everyone was wearing masks by then. Hers at first were rags, torn and folded from an old T-shirt. They passed. The pier and the beach were closed, and most of all the parking lots, but now and then someone jogged along the water's edge or threw a frisbee for a dog. She lay so still in the sand that seagulls walked right over her. "Really," she said, when she came back. She would have brought some shells from the beach, but there hadn't been any shells. She didn't go near the water. "Too many drunks still at the beach," she said. Too many drug addicts. Drunks and addicts she didn't know, who didn't know her. Still, she bought a few of them sandwiches from a convenience store, cans of something to drink. She was as contradictory as anyone. Everything moment by moment.

Her people at the camp minded her stuff, her blue tent and her tote bags full of clean and dirty clothes, the books she collected when she came across them offered free on a sidewalk. She helped her people and they helped her. Most of the books weren't worth reading, but she passed them along to anyone who wanted paper to write on or to wipe their ass. The bad books, she didn't care, and when now and then she found a treasure worth saving, she gave it to someone who would know its value, who might even read it to her aloud.

She had more trouble herself reading than she used to. Probably needed glasses. Teeth fixed too. She let the street clinic doctor look her over.

"Not too bad," the woman said. "You should move indoors."

Right. *Right?* She would have said so, too, ten years ago, to the Trinity visible now.

THE MARCH SWELLED and contracted and swelled again, sometimes moving slowly, sometimes fast, sweeping away her original companions, landing her with others. As the crowd left the street to pour into the park, she saw ahead an empty slab for sitting on. The kids could march all day and then some, but she still had to make her way back to camp. She sat down on the bright concrete bench, resisting the desire to lie, to curl up there, knowing that her policeman or another would come and move her on if she did. She lowered her chin and closed her eyes. One by one, to keep from falling asleep, she fingered the wooden beads wrapped on her wrist.

The thing about shelter is, she said to her brother and sister, you never know where you'll find it. You won't always recognize it. It's nothing like what these people say.

Our people, she asked them, do you know who they were?—but how could you? Even they didn't know. As rootless as you and me. Crossed oceans to escape their failures, their demons, crossed rivers and mountains and prairies to cash in on dreams. For what? Every generation more restless than the last. No knowledge of the land, the water, the air. No respect for the animals or trees. Far from their own dead and always scrabbling after whatever was out of reach.

The boy interrupted her to argue. Some of them came driven by hunger, by famine, he said, our ancestors too. Some came kidnapped, captured, bought and sold, in chains.

Yes, Trinity answered. But we're not them and even with almost no options our people still got to choose. We're an infection everywhere. Just like the disease. Our father's father, born in Tennessee before the Civil War, every son he made was born farther west, our father the last, in Colorado, before the War to End All Wars, until, finally, after the second one, us—all the way to the coast. No wonder we live on the street. It's the only just end for all of us. You'll see.

Hush, the sister said, and in the quiet that followed Trinity found her own sadness for their friends who had died, and for all the strangers who had also died and been killed, and for this day of mourning and celebration and protest, and for all the sorrows they knew were yet to come.

THE PARK WAS filling and overflowing, closing in around them on their bench, and at the far end, across the crowd, above the stage, a screen lit up. A voice screeched through the sound system before it softened. A man made a speech, a woman sang, a woman spoke, a band played, and Trinity rocked from side to side with whatever rhythm moved her, hearing words and without much effort continuing to ignore them. She no longer believed in the world in which such words had meaning. She saw the butterfly girl again, and the girl saw her and smiled as if remembering, directly at her, a great red smile, like Araceli's, and then the face of the tall Black boy beside her exploded, and the girl was splattered as if with bright crimson paint.

Sound stopped. People dropped, to concrete or grass, or spreading their arms, flopped flat on top of whoever was underneath. Others ran, careful at first not to trample, then not so much—all chaos and movement, muted.

Why could she not hear? Movement and color lost signification. She tasted orange in her mouth and felt grit against her cheek. She saw the spider, gold and black and striped like a tiger. She saw the policeman who had urged her off the ledge. She saw herself sitting on the ledge. Maybe she had stayed there. Maybe, after all, she had resisted him. Anything was possible. *Who goes on a cruise? Who flies to Italy?* Who were her people anyhow? Because of the virus, three of her friends had died. She wasn't meant to lose the house—but then she wasn't meant ever to have a house to begin with.

She wants the sun to come out, to reach her.

Like the people around her, she's flat on the ground.

She knows the name for the state of her mind and body—tonic immobility, not quite playing dead.

Later she will have a story to tell, another story. She will spend money on a room and take a friend and get a shower and watch the news to understand what was happening, what's happening now, what she's laid out frozen in the heart of.

THE FIRST SOUND she hears, when sound comes back, is a siren, sirens; then gradually voices, a moan, a scream, orders—police and EMTs everywhere, talking to people down on the ground, helping the living to their feet.

As soon as she can move, she will stand and walk away. No one will try to stop her. They will hardly notice her. No one will ask who she is or what she's seen.

What has she seen?

She's been alone a long time, in this life and in the lives that came before. Whatever has happened here had snuck up on her from behind, reached her under the radar, until she woke to this silent body, mute, muted. No one would ask her anything. What can she say?

She rolls herself up and, drawing her thin coat around herself, checks for her brother and sister, one at each hand. It's time to find shelter and a meal, to return to their tent and their treasures, watched over by one of their friends. She takes care of her friends and her friends take care of her. They're not alone. She finds friends everywhere.

The sky is getting pink. Too early for sunset, she thinks, then understands more time has passed than she knew.

Ready? she asks the others, and, *Yes,* they say, and together they get up from the concrete and brush her off, straighten her coat, and pick up her garland of ribbons and bruised flowers, making sure she's steady on her feet.

No one tries to stop them. No one asks who they are or whether they're hurt or what they've seen.

She puts the garland on her head and welcomes the slight sensation as the evening breeze sets a streamer dancing on her skin.

She wriggles her fingers and knows the weight of the beads on her wrist. She taps her forehead and cheeks, the back of her neck, her shoulders. She rubs her hands together, just to feel the pressure of one against the other.

Alive, she says to the brother, the sister, the last of her original people. Still alive.

This time, the boy says.

No matter how she ages, he will always be a boy.

Hush, says the sister.

Her favorite word.

Cat Sitting for a Ghost

HER NAME WAS Elizabeth but everyone called her Birdie. The nickname had started with her parents, who wanted her to go by Little Bit—like the Queen of England, they thought—but that was corrupted almost immediately by her brother, the source of all suffering and evil.

Birdie said this to the woman interviewing her, a somewhat well-known actress with a cat and a little house on a hill. What the job required was living in the house, feeding the cat, following a few simple rules. Basic, nothing too restrictive. Still, the actress seemed uncertain. She would be away for a month, maybe six weeks. The cat refused to show itself.

Birdie's references were spotty. Her first job, memorizing and performing the script on a bus tour to the mansions of stars, had come to her through a catering friend of her brother's. Next, she had worked as a personal assistant, a shopper, a driver, a chore whore. All that and not yet twenty-one.

"I used to have two cats," the actress said. "One of them ran off the last time I was out of town." She was reluctant but in urgent need. Her usual cat sitter was suddenly unavailable, and shooting would start in Istanbul in two days. Could Birdie do this, live up here in the hills for a month, follow the rules, be good to the cat?

Of course, yes. She wouldn't have come for the interview otherwise.

Her brother's catering friend had set her up with the interview. He wasn't her brother's friend anymore, but he still helped Birdie get gigs, and she won the actress over by reciting an excerpt from her star tour script, with every exaggerated inflection and several stupid jokes.

ALONE IN THE house the first night, the cat still not in evidence, Birdie settled in with the remote and the vast TV to watch *The Expanse* from beginning to end, all five seasons if she could stay awake that long. The hero, or anti-hero, whatever he was, reminded her of her brother, and as she watched Holden navigate that dystopic future, she wondered what it was about her brother that had caused her always to see him as the origin of evil. She had never been able to figure it out. She wanted him to be double, hero and anti- both. But no good side ever appeared.

In childhood games he had mostly played the tormentor to her victim. Faced with parental authority he had accused and forced her to defend. In acts of destruction he took the lead. He was master of secrets and first to install locks on his door. Not one lock. Multiple locks. As a child he killed her stuffed animals with electric cords and kitchen knives, and as an adolescent he lurked in the hall at night, staring at her from a distance she had never learned to penetrate. Even their parents knew there was something wrong with him, although they would never admit it, not to her. But sometimes she listened when they thought she couldn't hear.

She did what she could to get out of their house. First, the tour bus leafleting gig. It was true that her brother had helped her find that, but only so that when she was working he could harass her out on the street. Then the other jobs. Now the cat sit. She could have gone to college, probably, but college would not have freed her from him. Her parents insisted that she attend locally and live in their house. They couldn't afford more, not for two of them, or even for one, and they wouldn't risk taking out loans. They had almost lost the house in the 2008 crash. Birdie remembered her brother intensifying those days of crisis as he goaded and screeched. Never in public, only at home, at the dinner table, in the kitchen, in the living room in front of the TV. Whenever they were all together and one of the parents told him no. Birdie saw the structure of every episode clearly. Both adults had to be present and one had to reject some small request or claim. Then *kazam!* out came the demon. And the demon was still in him, all grown up and living at home, just like her. It was a relief to get away.

Holden, on the big TV, looked a little like her brother, although more muscular and handsome, but something other than the actor's appearance brought her brother to mind. Some moral unclarity, buried in the character's certainties, an absolute anger hiding in the struggle between heroism and denial—all that, but finally also hope. Holden, after all, was meant to be the good guy, utterly redeemed.

Birdie doubted redemption would be possible for her brother. She wondered daily when he would blow.

SHE HAD PUT food down for the cat but she had still not seen the creature. Teddy, its name was. A black and white not quite tuxedo cat, with one blue and one green eye. The actress had described it and its habits in extensive detail. It liked the back deck, stalked squirrels and birds from its perch there without success. Occasionally it leapt down to the yard and disappeared into the jungle lower on the slope, rarely for more than an hour or two. Sometimes the actress heard shrieks of conflict, and Teddy would soon reemerge, only slightly ruffed up. "He's lost a claw," she said, "but he's never been injured. No cat has ever defeated him."

Maybe, Birdie thought, but she knew that appearances and fighting boys were likely to deceive. Meanwhile, the cat remained invisible, except in photographs on a glass bookshelf, side by side with another cat, the missing tortoiseshell, and shots of the actress in various roles.

Face to face, the actress seemed nothing like the characters Birdie had seen her play. Just an ordinary person with a cat and a worry. No glamour, no meanness, no pathological schemes.

"I was an innocent in that first part," the actress told her when she noticed her looking at the photographs. "A girl no older than you. Younger in fact. Surrounded by power-mad conspirators. A pawn in their game until she learned to think like a queen."

ALL THROUGH SCHOOL Birdie's brother had been a weirdo and everybody knew it, unresponsive to kindness, to people who wanted to be his friend, and he rejected enemies also, refusing to engage. The mean kids didn't even bother to bully him. Like everyone else, they left him alone. Sometimes he attached himself to one or another person, a sort of favorite he would hang out with for a while, until whatever it was between them collapsed and the former favorite returned to the pack, bearing tales. Birdie had heard some of these stories, second hand. Acts of cruelty to insects and small mammals. Violence to someone's pet. Minor thefts, undetectable and without value. Strange obsessions—blood oaths, scarifications, territorial markings with fire and his own urine and semen and shit. She thought the rumors were probably exaggerated. She thought he made those short-lived friendships for no other reason than to set these rumors in motion. She wondered what he had told the catering guy who got her the job on the bus. *My kid sister, as weird as I am, weirder.* The guy had never told her, not even the night they hooked up.

TEDDY HAD HIS own door, a flap between the kitchen and the deck. When the wind blew, the flap clapped and at first Birdie thought the cat had finally come in, but when she got up to look she found no sign of him. The wind spooked her a bit and she pulled the actress's cashmere afghan protectively around herself to curl into a corner of the couch and start another episode. The show was spooky too she thought but she wasn't sure it was meant to be. All those strung-out long-boned Belters and the murderous blue goo, the drifting lights and crystal-forming ectoplasm or whatever, protomolecule and its ongoing deadly consequence. The wind howled—literally, up on this hillside—and she heard coyotes, celebrating a kill.

Before she went to bed, every night she put food out on the deck for the cat, and every morning it was gone—eaten by a feral, maybe, or squirrels, or mice. Any creature but Teddy.

ONE OF THE actress's simple rules was that Birdie was not to leave the house until the cat showed himself and then she was to shut him in if she had to leave and was not to leave him shut in alone any longer than three hours until he was so thoroughly used to her that she could count on him to come and go and still return.

She had been alone in the house for five days and was running out of fresh food. She would have to order a delivery. The actress had prepared for that, left her a phone set up with Venmo to use instead of her own. Everything she could need was on it. Chewy. Vet. Car service. Whole Foods.

Another of the simple rules was that there should be no guests. Not until Teddy came home and had thoroughly accepted Birdie. After that, guests would be all right. Even overnight. Whatever. Just no strangers. Only people Birdie knew.

Birdie didn't think she cared. She liked the solitude. She liked binge watching *The Expanse* and browsing the actress's bookshelves, discovering odd treasures. She liked sitting out on the deck, looking down the hillside into other yards and the narrow roads that wound through the canyon, so different from the gridded flatland she had grown up in.

But she did care. After five days she was getting squirrelly. She almost called her brother but ordered food instead and tried flirting with the masked delivery man, which worked for a few minutes, but not for long. What he wanted was a tip. Next, she tried music, wearing headphones, dancing with herself. (Music without headphones was against the rules.) Dancing, she peeled off her clothes, all but the black bikini panties, and staring at her reflection, near naked in the deck doors, conjured her first lover, a woman older than herself who had known what to do to move her frightened hungry body to response. She let the phantom woman squeeze her breasts and bite her nipples and felt the flesh tingle and contract. She reached for her pubes and holding herself loosely, gazed at her reflection and sent the phantom away. She imagined balls there, cupped in her palm, until she could feel them, young and taut and almost hairless, a hard cock rising in her hand as if it were her own. As she worked it with her mind where it filled her grip, in sensation she thickened and overflowed—not another's sex entering and filling, not her own receiving either, just an absolute pulse of interior flesh—not male, not female, not neither, not both. Nameless, before separation.

In the aftermath, she stared at herself in the doors' glass, coming up lost from waves of double consciousness. Naked, she almost looked like her brother. Narrow hips, flat chest. Not quite flat. Not flat enough, and otherwise lacking. Nine minutes younger. Nothing had ever been fair.

She realized suddenly then how exposed she must be, a bony girl standing naked and touching herself in front of the glass. She stepped back and found the afghan and wrapped herself in it. No one to see her out there anyway. Squirrels and coyotes and maybe a feral cat.

She had still not finished *The Expanse*—it was a marathon, really—and Teddy had not come home.

Later that night, as she put food out again on the deck, she wondered for the first time whether there really was a cat—had ever been a cat other than the ferals. Suddenly the actress with all her rules seemed peculiar, even cruel—as weird and possibly dangerous as Birdie's brother. The wind had not let up and in the morning when she checked the bowl and found it emptied, as usual, in the distance she saw black smoke that indicated fire. She turned a radio on to find out where the fire was and which way it was heading and left it on, half listening to a call-in show. She wanted to call in herself, just to hear her own voice being heard, responding and responded to. Instead she went into the actress's workout room, rode the exercise bike, and pumped and pushed and pulled on the rowing machine, with eyes shut pretending to cut across the surface of an endless placid lake. The only lake she had ever seen in real life was the lake at Echo Park—nothing like the lake she was crossing now, in the wilderness and utterly alone.

THREE DAYS LATER the fire still burned. It was far from her, far from the actress's house, from the canyon, from this hillside, but smoke filled the air, the sky often red, especially at sunset. At first she had watched stars from up here, even shooting stars, more stars than she ever could see from down below. Now there was nothing—even the moon, though visible, shrouded. On the radio call-in show people who sounded as weird to her as her brother prayed for rain. Firefighters were flying in from neighboring counties and prisons. She started watching the news on television, just to see the images. One night she forgot to put food out for the cat and woke abruptly, remembering, hours before dawn, as if a cry from him had reached her.

She got up and filled a clean bowl and a clean plate and took them out to the deck. The smoke was thicker than ever and smelled of sage and eucalyptus. She waited for the sun to rise, the sky to show its color, but it was still dark when her phone rang. It was her brother. She decided to answer. He was worried about her, he said. Everybody missed her at home.

"Tell them I'm fine," she said. "It's smoky here but the fire is far away."

He wanted to come up and see her. He didn't know the address. She would never allow him to be here. There was too much glass. She told him she couldn't have visitors until the cat came home.

"There's no cat?" he said. "You're cat sitting and there's no cat?" He started laughing.

"There're lots of plants to water," she told him. It was true there were plants. She had been neglecting them out of fear of overwatering. She had killed too many plants with water in her time.

"And you call me the weirdo," he said, still laughing.

Most of us are ghouls, she thought, but he was laughing so hard at her that she hung up and didn't answer when he called her back. She thought about texting his former friend, the dude who got her the job. He sort of knew the actress, after all, and maybe knew where Birdie was, so maybe breaking the rule against guests didn't entirely apply to him. It was time to call out again for food, too, another person to possibly talk to.

She had not let the actress know that Teddy had not come home. She would have told her if asked, of course, but she had not heard from the actress at all. The actress had said to expect this. Not to bother her with anything. "Not even if the house burns down."

Birdie had laughed at this at the time, but now it didn't seem funny. The fire was not coming her way but it was also not dying out, and she began to wonder whether she should let her employer know about Teddy's continued absence. She couldn't have expected him to be missing for so long. Maybe she would have some good idea for how to lure him in, or where to look. Except, of course, that in order to go looking, Birdie would have to leave the house.

HER BROTHER WAS weird in other ways. He got obsessed with people, real people and public figures. He stalked whatever object of obsession he was stuck on in person and online. When they were children it was a little girl up the street, the boy brilliant in math, a checker at their local Von's, a pretty woman in the choir at church—people singled out as if at random, then studied: followed them, drew them, even shot them with a phone if he got the chance. He would dress himself up as whatever person he was studying. He would make up stories. In the games when he tormented Birdie she was often playing one of those parts—the little girl, the brilliant boy, the cashier, the woman wearing choir robes assembled from their mother's dresses and skirts. If they were caught she took the blame. His punishment would have been worse.

When they were older he grew more careful, acting out only in his mind. Or in his sketchbooks, she suspected, alone in his room with his door triple locked and music pounding through the walls to mask whatever he was up to. He left her out of his games.

As soon as they finished high school, he went to work, first with the catering, then in an old folks home. The hours were good, four days on, three days off. The four days on were a relief to her; he was absent from her life for a hundred hours straight. But then he came back, each week more sullen and brooding. His bag when he came home bulged with more than laundry. She thought maybe he was stealing drugs from the old people. Or their phones, or little treasures, the kinds of things no one would miss but themselves. He was like that. He would take what you valued for no other reason than that you valued it—for the joy he would feel in knowing that its loss would cause you pain. His door was always locked. There were locks on his bedroom windows, too. He did his own laundry and vacuumed his own room, every week as soon as he got home, before he even ate or showered or slept. He trusted no one, least of all Birdie and their parents.

That night when she hung up on him, morning, whatever, and didn't answer again, he had barraged her with photos and texts. She had muted notifications and soon went back to bed, so she didn't see the messages until late the next day. It was as if suddenly she, or the actress, had become his object of obsession. He must have stayed up the rest of his night composing this assemblage. She told herself at first that she wouldn't read his messages, but sat up against the pillows and couldn't stop looking, reading. The words were almost innocent, often framed in quotation marks, with attribution to some renowned or notorious person: Nietzsche, Emily Dickinson, Charlie Manson, Julian Assange. The photographs, though, and their juxtapositions, were more disturbing. They showed details of his body. Not sex parts, but skin and metal and scars and tattoos. She had no idea he had so many tattoos. So many scars either. And piercings. She only ever saw his body covered, nothing showing but the star on the back of one hand and the chess piece on the other, which matched her own, in mirror image—done together on their twelfth birthday, *his* twelfth birthday, the nine minutes between them spanning the midnight hour. Not showing his body was another of his eccentricities, always buttoned to the wrist, to the neck. Now she saw why. Barbed wire, knives and guns, a swastika, a dripping heart. He sent photos of his room: walls painted a dark almost black red, dead roses in a bourbon bottle, a handful of closeups of books on a shelf: *Mein Kampf, The Hero With a Thousand Faces, The Unabomber Manifesto, Atlas Shrugged*; a wall of framed headshots of men she mostly didn't recognize until he also sent their names (Richard Spencer, Anders Behring Breivik, Patrick Crusius, Santino William Logan, James Holmes, Dylann Roof), and between the names and their faces she got the drift. She almost stopped there and would have missed the last photo: laid out on his bed, an arsenal—hand gun, rifle, machine gun, belts filled with bullets, a mountain of clips. Then one more image, a sunny video, arriving live: a tortoiseshell cat on a white hospital bed, serenely licking its paws, while the oldest woman Birdie had ever seen smiled at the camera and waved.

She threw the phone down and got out of bed, went out onto the deck, breathed the morning smoke, and tried to reason with herself. He had clearly gone to work. He would be away from home the next four days. She could call their parents, tell them what was hidden in his room. She could sound the alarm. But the cat, even more than the guns, spooked her. She was irrationally certain it was the actress's cat, the one that had gone missing before Birdie ever met her, before she came to stay in this house. What did he mean, sending that to her? All the carefully staged images and their associations to violence, followed by that sunlit cat?

Was it a threat? To her? To the actress? To the old woman? To the cat in the video, or to the other one, the cat Birdie was responsible for and still had never seen?

Baffled, she did nothing. She showered and dressed, played with the actress's makeup and called out for food. She kept the delivery man in conversation for nearly half an hour and when he finally left she added a big tip to the Venmo payment to compensate for the tips he'd likely lost in the delay. He was a boy, actually, more than a man, younger even than she was, and he didn't have much of interest to offer, but still it was good to hear a voice in the doorway, in the room with her, to see another body in all its dimensions, to smell another being, even dangerously to breathe his breath, to know he would leave some molecules behind. When she gave him a glass of orange juice, her hand skimmed his hand. She would have liked to touch him, but didn't want to flirt. She didn't want to scare him or seduce him, just wanted to know in that moment with all her senses another human person present and alive in the world.

By the time she finally let him go she had convinced herself that she had overreacted to her brother's messages. The photos were probably not taken in his room at all. How would she know? She had not been allowed in his room since before he installed the locks. Maybe even the tattoos and piercings weren't his own. The shot of guns on the bed, like all the others, could have come off the internet. Even the books on the shelf, the rogue's gallery. Smoke and mirrors, she thought. Another illusion. David Copperfield, too, had been one of his childhood heroes.

If she had a way of checking, she told herself, only the cat and the old lady would turn out to be real.

THAT NIGHT SHE dreamed about her first lover, the older woman, as if she was lying in the bed with her, a leg between her legs, long black hair falling across her face. She was still the most beautiful woman—the most beautiful human—Birdie had ever kissed or touched. And strange—silent about herself, her present, her past. Elusive. She seemed not to know her own beauty, and the not knowing was part of what made her beautiful. In the dream the woman whispered to her, words Birdie couldn't remember but which her skin understood. She woke to moonlight, blue and bright, and out the window, without getting up, clear stars. When she slept again, she felt a weight on her body, between her legs, dreaming she was dreaming still, then woke enough to freeze, to fear—the delivery boy, the catering friend, maybe even her brother. She was awake and the weight on her was big—another being in the bed, another breath, not moving, only sleeping.

When she finally stirred, just a little, it bolted and leapt away. The cat, she thought, knew at last. The cat had come home. Teddy, or maybe even the other one.

She got up to look and didn't find him but stood on the deck awhile in the moonlight, and after she slept again and woke in the morning to orange sky and smoke, she concluded that his presence and the stars and moon, like the woman, her lover, had been just another dream.

SHE HAD ALMOST reached the end of *The Expanse*—she had detoured several times—when she realized the origin of the first lover's haunting was the slight resemblance she bore to the Thai-French actress playing the sci-fi show's elusive Julie Mao—long thick black hair, sharp cheekbones, dark watchful eyes, and the character, like Birdie's lover, out of reach. Righteous and brave. Attractor for desire and mystery. Ultimately, maybe, a promise of salvation.

Some sort of salvation.

But what salvation was her dream-self looking for?

She was trapped in her life, she thought, and more to the point, trapped in this house, and if Teddy came home, she would be obliged to trap him, too. What was the point of all this trapping? She was not exactly restless. She didn't think so. This was about something else. Magic. Transformation. Or illusion. She was only twenty years old, after all.

To stop thinking, she started to clean. Cleaning was also part of her job. She had been neglecting this responsibility. The regular housecleaner got time off when the actress was out of town.

Working from room to room, wearing headphones, she found several concentrations of black and white cat hair—in dust bunnies under the bed and in every corner, on a pillow in a nook where she herself never sat, on the seat of the swivel chair in the actress's office, on the black and gray and tan New-Mexico-style throw rug that protected bare feet from cold slate beside the wall of glass sliding doors.

The house had been freshly cleaned the day before she arrived. The actress told her this when she outlined what Birdie would need to take care of and what she could ignore.

So the housekeeper was sloppy, or the actress lied, or there was no housekeeper at all, or Teddy had been home all along. Coming and going while she slept, or while she watched TV. She wondered what else she might have missed. The cat in the bed with her was, after all, not a dream.

HER BROTHER FINALLY found her, showed up one night, covered in blood.

"I'm dead," he told her. "You're free."

The dream disturbed her, not only because it was ghoulish, but because she was uncertain whether it spoke a wish or a fear or somehow a reality.

For the first time in days she turned the television on and saw news of a shooting downtown in the middle of a demonstration. Seventeen dead and injured. The shooter in custody, or maybe also dead. The police hadn't released the shooter's name, but there was a photo of the officer who had brought him down.

Birdie started to shake. It was—or the photo resembled—the woman who had been her lover, her personal Julie Mao. She didn't recognize the officer's name but she knew the lover had most likely not used her real name when they hooked up. They had met online when Birdie was so young as almost to be illegal.

It was impossible, then, she thought—if the officer on TV really was her lover—that the shooter could have been her brother. Too much coincidence. In a city of four million people? In greater L.A., twenty?

She called her brother and he didn't answer. She called her mother. Nothing.

She didn't know what to wish for.

THE BETTER NEWS that day was that the fire was finally contained, the smoke receding. A good rain was coming, followed by wind. The air would clear.

That night, as she lay awake, hoping that someone in her family would finally return one of her calls, the cat—Teddy, the black and white tuxedo cat with one blue and one green eye—strolled in and looked at her contemplatively before hopping up on the bed and circling itself a few times, then settling on a spot to knead, dropped and curled and slept, close but not on top of her. When she heard it purring she was almost asleep herself. Then she realized the purr was her phone, vibrating.

She reached for it and answered without speaking.

"Birdie?" he said. "Are you there?"

He laughed and showed her his hands, his face, his chest—naked and hairless and covered in ink. "You thought it was me, didn't you?"

He held a razor blade up to the eye of the phone. "That wasn't me," he said. "But this is. Don't look away."

He pressed the blade to his flesh. Not to slash, as for an instant she feared, but to make a new mark. His inner arm was crosshatched with a meshwork of delicate scars. Tiny beads of blood rose on his pale skin. He brought his arm to his mouth and licked—or sucked or drank, she couldn't tell. But she could feel it, his mouth on the soft flesh of her inner forearm, the salt of his blood on her tongue.

He was talking to her still, but Birdie wasn't listening. She was listening to the purring cat instead. She was thinking. The cat had returned and seemed to accept her. In fact, had been accepting her for a long time, if invisibly, had been sleeping with her in the bed, now had finally shown himself face to face. She was not obliged to shut him in and she was not trapped in this house any longer. She could go out. She could invite someone, anyone, over.

"Little Bit," her brother said. "Turn your camera on. I know where you are."

He had lit his call perfectly, taking care that she could see every detail, his skin, his blade, his blood.

She put the phone down and got up from the bed, and pulling on the actress's persimmon silk kimono, letting it hang open over her naked skin, she left her brother's rambling voice behind. She walked across the Berber carpet and cold slate, onto the woven New Mexico rug, and out. She stood on the weather-worn deck and looked up at the sky and the stars.

Mark me, she thought, or said. To the sky, to the stars.

To the lover and the shooter.

To the ghost cat and the ferals.

Scar me. Burn me. Set me free.

In the future perhaps he will have another chance

The Man

He attracts attention. How? He is clean. His hair is long. He has taken off his clothes. No one can read him. He is not young. He is not old. He is not white. He is not Black. He is an immigrant perhaps, or an original inhabitant, brown, golden, hairless except for the long black hair. No one can see his eyes. He has covered his eyes with a blindfold. A black scarf tied around his head. Or someone else has covered his eyes. He is not quite naked, not as naked as at first he appeared, but wrapped in a pale loin cloth, just sufficient to cover him, his essential privacy, his sex. His wrists bear marks of binding.

Caroline lived in Iowa

in a town that no longer had commercial prospects. It was only the second town she'd ever lived in and she wanted to get away. One night she dreamed of a pearl, a man named Kains, and a shoreline, a crashing sea, and crows, she counted them, sixty-seven, seventy-seven, until they flew away. When she awoke she went outside to her porch and watched the sun rise and smelled the lilacs, all in bloom because it was already May. Another year had passed of not leaving, not getting on that highway, not heading for that shoreline, her ninth year in that town, that shrinking town, that village, and still she had no sense of how to move, to uproot, to take herself off. Until suddenly she did.

Voices in the Crowd

In the present he has no luck. The clouds are forming, thunder written—future storms already here. Perhaps he deserves something kinder? He deserves nothing. Will they help him even so? Have they found the heart of mercy? Another opportunity waits at every corner. Chance sets him up—succeed or fail.

From the safety of her car

Caroline saw the naked, blindfolded man, saw something beautiful, the circle of space opening around him. She sat transfixed, by the spectacle or by his beauty. Nothing happened. The circle grew. The man spread his arms. He might have been speaking. Or singing. She couldn't tell from where she sat. She waited for something to happen, anything. For the police to pull up. For someone to intervene. To take the man by the hand. To try to speak to him. To give him a shirt, or a coat. She has waited three hours. She will wait while the sky goes from cloudless blue to stormy gray and back again. She will wait while the sun lights windows gold before disappearing beyond the tall buildings to the west. She will wait into nightfall. No one will be in the street but the man and herself. All others move, pass through. Only they are rooted here, she and he.

The Palm Tree and the Jacaranda

I'm more beautiful, says the jacaranda.

I'm iconic, says the palm tree.

People come to this corner to look at me, she says.

Me, he says.

You have no color, the jacaranda says. You're shaggy. You shed all over the sidewalk. The only people who stop at this corner on your account are street cleaners. You obscure my view.

You're so vain, says the palm tree.

Of course I'm vain, she says. I'm beautiful. You would be too.

I've been here longer than you have, he says. I've always been here.

Not always, she says.

What do you want from me? he asks.

Nothing, she says. I want you to be tidier, I want you to move, you're crowding me. You could be on that other corner over there, with your brother. He's more handsome than you are. You would be handsomer from a distance.

You know I can't move, right? the palm tree says.

Nonsense, says the jacaranda. The palm frond cleaners move you boys all the time. They take you down.

You'd miss me, the palm tree says.

Fat chance, she says.

Who would you talk to?

Myself, she says. And the people who come to gawk at me. I can sing, you know, she adds.

I didn't know.

You haven't been listening.

All I ever hear from you is complaining. You'd stop listening too. I do enjoy just looking at your flowers.

Hmm, she says.

I like you just as much when the flowers fall, the palm tree says.

When what?

You're not so tidy then yourself.

When do my flowers fall?

Every year. Have you forgotten? You slime the sidewalks.

That can't be true, she says. This is the land of eternal springtime.

Only in your mind, the palm tree says.

I don't remember any other time.

That's what I'm here for, the palm tree says. That's why you need me.

Hmm, she says again. She rustles her branches, her purple flowers. A petal falls, and then another. She begins to sing.

A driver passing by

came here god knows when seduced by images golden sunshine balmy breezes seagulls on blue skies you know how it looks to everyone anywhere else the glamour the beauty of lights at night spread out all over the city horizon to horizon a human fucking galaxy that when you live here you come to realize you never actually see. The way you get stuck in your little habits your favorite route, Pico, La Cienega, the 405, whatever. When do you ever go up into the hills and take in the bigger picture? It's not what I thought it would be, that's the truth, and I can't shake the disappointment, the whole place reeks of it, the pink metallic air, the rationed water, the dried-up grass, the burning eucalyptus trees. When the fires started that's when I got that disappointment's part of the draw, the fascination. I knew it would never live up to the image, the dream, I knew it would break my heart. When the fires started I knew I'd always known. This broken heart is what I came here for, this and to watch things burn. But the fires were only a spectacle and another disappointment. I watched from down below, the orange sky filling with smoke and ash, the air too heavy to breathe. I asked for this, I know, but what was in it for me? It just set me up to dream again, to yearn again for another place that can't live up to its promises, New York or Paris maybe, maybe Barcelona. I've been reading about Barcelona lately. I can already taste it.

•

Pink Magnolia

At the corner of a house with a pink magnolia, tall and blooming and shedding its petals, a man stood listening.

He had been a man with a job and now he was the man who had lost it.

The smell of bacon wafted through the window, and laughter too, loud and silly and young.

—I don't want it.

—You have to take it.

—Says who?

When he showed up for work and they told him no, they didn't want him, he kicked the trash basket and slammed the door and then drove around the city until he was nearly out of gas. Driving around, he saw things. Heard things. Voices.

The sprinkler hose was coiled on the grass and water sprayed in crystal droplets.

He had come to see his sister, but she wasn't here.

A bird, red, flew into the florid tree.

—If you don't, I can't make it home. I can't go home with this. You know that.

—Then don't go home.

—Are you crazy?

Instead he found his mother, taking care of the kids, feeding them breakfast after school.

Suddenly there was thunder.

He wanted to tell her about the man downtown standing naked on the sidewalk. He wanted to tell her he had lost his job and didn't know why, that after they told him he just drove around. He wanted to show her the red bird exploding out of the pale pink tree.

He couldn't tell her anything.

Someone closed the window.

She would side with them, with the others, with his boss, or his former boss, with Jennifer, who didn't want him anymore either, even with the dog.

—I'm telling you, stay here.

And then there was rain.

A woman walking hates the heat

that rises off the asphalt and fills the air with burned tar, hates the smog that greets her lungs and nose and eyes on late afternoons like this one when she leaves her air-conditioned building for the street, hates the street, the noise, the cars, the traffic, the people—yes, that's true, she hates the people, especially the young ones in their shorts and perfect tans, but not all the young ones, really be honest, some of them are beautiful and kind and she loves their beautiful kindness, the way they hide inside the noise and chaos, their near invisibility, like herself she thinks, herself the way she's always been, lost in the crowd, finding her way to her parking lot, her car. She loves the music on the last quiet station on the dial, loves that on the road she's alone at last, enclosed in glass and plastic and steel, in listless traffic, in the mind she has forgotten with everything that came before—the world she has forgotten, the playgrounds of her childhood, the tide pools and her father's hands, her mother's breath, her voice, the children on the street who played outside at night without fear, in that time of innocence and ignorance. She would not choose to remember any of it, even if she could. She would not remember one thing, good or bad, that has ever happened to her or anything she's ever seen or done and not done. Memory is overrated, she thinks. Although maybe there was a day at the beach, a wave, a swell, an undercurrent—wet, salt, cold, blue. A blue she would remember, a sky that blue, that green, a flower, a bucket, an ice plant, a room, a table, a meal, white plates and candles that same sea blue, sea green. On the freeway, a pinkening darkening sky, the same route every day, the sky each day new—this sky, this hour, her only life. She has no way to think about it. Everything else was function. She prefers her life without words. Without words she is no one. She prefers being no one.

The other one, the one called Caroline—

still sitting in her car, watching the nearly naked man, waiting, but for what?—is many things to many people. They make stories about her, big and little, a different Caroline for each, or many Carolines, and even for her, this one called Caroline, the many Carolines are fictions, fabrications, as she is herself. In other words, nobody's home. Nobody's ever been home. Still, there is a life that likes some things and dislikes others. Coffee, chocolate, cheese, a fresh tomato, digging in the dirt, the coming of rain, the end of rain, the singing birds, the cat, any cat but also the cat she thinks of as her own now, although she knows he can't be, the cat the same countless cats as the countless Carolines, and even though the cat's life has not yet been so long or various, the principle is the same, driven by liking and disliking, call of the mouse, the squirrel, the wild, and flight from rain and dogs. The cat likes his freedom and so does she, and every other she, future or left behind, unknown. Known, she can never be freedom, that force of the wild, would be only kept in a box, and even in the box, those boxes, would be traceless, always escaping, escaped—she cannot be kept, even now, in these moments, these hours of watching the man, about whom everyone who has seen him will have been making a story, a box to shut him into, to put him safely away.

(In Syracuse, she hears on the radio, they're culling the deer who roam the city. *Who*, not *that*. Praise the mothers. *Failure and flawlessness.* The answer is no. Drive into the wreck. Language is a body. *How does a body speak?*)

If she were a fiction, which she is and has to be, she would have something more to offer here, in this her final moment—a chocolate to melt in the mouth, a coffee to savor, a tomato to bite into and break between her teeth, and his. This is what fictions do. They smell the rain, the fire, they chase the mouse. They get out of the car and embrace the man. They take him home. They clothe him and feed him and bind up his wounds. They remove his blindfold and receive his words. They listen and taste. They touch. They burn.

Enough now, she says, to no one.

Crazy

Copper stain on sanded pine shining through layers of clear polyurethane, a floor as brilliant and artificial as any other polished thing she'd seen in this city.

—I want you to quit your job. I want you to say no to that man. Finally. I mean it.

The potted palms and lilies at least were real but grew in a medium as distant from soil as she was from Tennessee.

—I've put so much into that place. Half my life, she said.

An overloaded pickup truck barreled down the street, screeching, scattering debris as it rounded the corner, scaring children and dogs. A man ran after it, shouting and shaking his fist, like someone in a cartoon, a thought bubble over his head: *Motherfucker.*

The sky that was supposed to be blue was a dull steel, waiting for rain or sunset, it didn't seem to know.

—It's not half your life. It's a drop in the bucket. One band of a rainbow. Get over it. Get over him.

—You don't know what you're talking about.

Motherfucker, the thought bubble read. *Why did you miss me?*

Out there somewhere birds were singing, but there didn't seem to be any trees.

The dogs in the street kept barking, until the children began throwing rocks.

—I know that working for him in that environment oppresses you. I know it's time to cut loose. Be free.

Maybe they were recordings of birds.

An acrid odor blew in on a breeze, followed by the scent of dust, and eucalyptus and fire.

—You'll never get it. You can't understand.

—Fine. I don't get it. But you talk like a woman abused in a bad relationship, trapped only because she's unwilling to walk out.

She closed the window and saw the glass in need of washing.

The driver was on his way to see his sweetheart, a bouquet of daffodils on the torn seat beside him, the radio playing Patsy Cline.

"Crazy," she sang. "Crazy for loving you."

Buffalo

When she was young she knew a man—younger, many men, but in this instance, one man—whose name or nickname was Buffalo. Buffalo Bill or Buffalo Bob, she can't remember anymore, it was that long ago and a whole lot of cities in between. Buffalo. What she knew about the word was that there used to be and maybe still were buffalo in Golden Gate Park. It was in San Francisco that she knew that man. She didn't know him well, knew some of his friends better. But he was the one she always remembered—built like the shaggy haired wild ox of the prairie, big and short and broad in the chest and the paunch. Maybe more paunch than a buffalo, which after all were lean in the belly. Maybe he came on to her, or into her, in a Russian bath. It was so long ago, what can she know? She had moved on since then, moved away, back and forth, for decades. She had lived in Ohio and Iowa and Massachusetts and New York, Pennsylvania and Virginia, and—was that all?—Oregon, too, as well as in northern California again, until finally, full circle, she came home.

She is not interested anymore in difficulties of language, does not care one iota or give one fig about foxes or lazy dogs, is not quick or brown or jumping, but the jingling bells she wore today must have proven to someone somewhere her value on this earth.

San Francisco was the only place she ever saw a buffalo. They're extinct, she thinks, were extinct even then, although some were kept living in the park. Or maybe they are not extinct? Maybe they came back with the wolves. Back to the Plains. Back with the Native peoples, who understand them. Understand them the way she understands, say, a dog. Dogs are smaller than buffalos, and probably softer. But how would she know? People, Native people, in the Dakotas probably, or Kansas, maybe know about the softness of buffalo. And the taste of the meat. She ate the meat once herself, tasted it, at Knott's Berry Farm, when she was a little girl. Knott's Berry Farm probably wasn't there anymore either. She doesn't know, she would have to look it up. If she had time. But what will it matter? Everything that had ever been in her world was gone or vanishing, and she isn't even all that old. Old but not that old. It was just that the world changed faster than anyone ever said it would when she was young—when they gave the impression that all things were stable, that losing a house to the wrecking ball was anomaly, that buffalo disappearing from the wild was, as a loss, exceptional, an aberration. Not in the normal course of events. Not the way things actually are.

She would have been a zebra, if she could, loved the stripes and black and white, the flicking tail, the lazy way of life on a savannah, the occasional desperate run from a lion, the jolt of fear that would set her off, the little sidestep, the quiet before, the excited shriek, and most of all the end, the catch, the kill—down, down, into the wild grass, to ground—until amen.

She wonders whether that man whose name was Buffalo—Dick maybe or even Tom or Harry?—wonders whether that man can still be alive. She was a good deal younger than he was back then. He would be a nonagenarian now, at least, maybe more than a hundred years old. More likely he was history, like the animal whose name he bore. She sees them sometimes on the computer screen where she watches movies and TV. Not that she watches westerns much—watched—more likely science fiction. That would be something, to see a buffalo on *Star Trek*, maybe, or *Battlestar Galactica*. Imagine, a buffalo out there in space, flying around, maybe learning to speak. Channeling its story to some heroic but puny human—

She hates tea, drank coffee all her life, lots of it, more when she still drank vodka and gin, less as she grew older, but still enjoys a thrill, painting the face this morning, the red lips, the thickened lashes, the contrast to the white of her hair, her image in a mirror—the jingling of her bracelets, the quickening pulse, the bliss of celebration and protest, of bodies and music, and even now, the slackening, the laxity of surrender, zeroing in on the end of things, of time, of herself.

You killed me, the sci-fi buffalo says. *You brought me to an end. You, pale European person, came and stole the land and subordinated the peoples and animals and pretended you owned it and them and us and you go on pretending. What's your reward? Pandemic and collapse of the biosphere. The end of your line. We who laugh last laugh best. You think you're really going to send us into space? A molecule here, a DNA chain there? No way, José. I am the creature I always was. Big and brute and wise and, above all, alive. Did that man rape you in that Russian bath? Don't blame the buffalo. That was pure human. Did some random angry white man shoot unrepentant into a motley crowd and take you out with a gun? Get over it. The whole world collapses. Every world bleeds out. Even this one that you call your own. Especially this one. Bells are ringing. Counting down. One hundred seconds on the doomsday clock. Are you ready? No need to wait. Come along with us. You're welcome with us anytime. A big old herd of shaggy buffalo storming through the sky.*

All her life she has loved purple, douses her body now in lilac and lavender, sometimes rose or sage, still plays poker late into the night, even old, even tired, online with old men, their muse, a favorite, knowing how she jangles in their dreams, quivering, their zest, their fox, all silver and gold, for life.

She doesn't know how to answer him after this rant. Him? Maybe it's a she-buffalo that speaks to her this way. A buffalo cow. Even more exploited than the hairy male. Milked. There had been buffalo milk, too, at that place of her childhood, and buffalo cheese, and cowboys with pistols and bandannas pretending to rob the train she rode that day with her mother and uncle and cousin. In the land of the Wild West, in that fantasy in which she had been a child. Worlds away. Time long gone. Petering out now. *One-minute warning,* the buffalo says. It makes the hundred seconds counting down toward the end of human life on earth seem a long, long possibility. Adios, then, she thinks. Says. Shouts. Adios.

And still a few seconds more. Can she not find one word to say for herself? — because there must be time for this, a final chance, no deception, forgetting nothing, jumping over contradiction, no more kicking the can down the road, no quitting, just one last leap after the next exacting detail, a victory over infinite zero — *all will be well* — one more breath — *all manner of thing* — one, last, more —

Acknowledgments

Many thanks are due the generous readers and editors who selected and published the following stories: "Eudora Loved Her Life" in *Cincinnati Review*, "A Vampire Story?" (as "Ursula and Will") in *The Missouri Review*, "Dangerous" in *Always Crashing*, "In Absence" at *Kenyon Review Online*, "Agency" in *Orca*, "In the future perhaps he will have another chance" at *Vol. 1 Brooklyn*, and "Buffalo" at *The Blood Pudding*.

A handful of quotations and borrowings appear in these stories, gratefully acknowledged here: The reference to "the poet" in "Dangerous" is to Terrance Hayes, and to his poem "American Sonnet for the New Year" (*The New Yorker*, January 7, 2019). In "Pack Rat, All Will Be Well," the quoted passage on pack rats is from Jill Lepore, *These Truths: A History of the United States* (W.W. Norton, 2018, pp. 7-8). The widely quoted lines from Julian of Norwich are adapted here from Julian of Norwich, *Showing of Love*, as translated by Julia Bolton Holloway (The Liturgical Press, 2003, p. 37). Caroline's parenthetical thoughts toward the end of "In the future perhaps he will have another chance" owe their genesis and combination to words of the poets Jules Gibbs and Rachel Eliza Griffiths offered in an online reading hosted by Northshire Bookstore Saratoga on May 11, 2021.

Special appreciation also goes to Deborah Bogen and Jeff Oaks for the delightful writing provocations that inspired "Dangerous," "Buffalo," and passages that found their way into "Cul-de-Sac."

I am happy to express my thanks to the Virginia Center for the Creative Arts, not only for the stay that grew several of these stories from small seeds, but for the many previous occasions of VCCA's hospitality and support.

To Deborah Attwood Morris, dear friend and spirit sister, thank you for the use of "3 Planets 2011" as the cover art.

Finally, my undying appreciation goes to Christine Kelly and Danilo Thomas of Baobab Press for their enthusiastic reception and thoughtful work in bringing *The Gunman and the Carnival* into the world.

Great gratitude to all.

Catherine Gammon is author of the novels *Isabel Out of the Rain, Sorrow, China Blue,* and *The Martyrs, The Lovers,* and of the early story collection *Beauty and the Beast.* Her work has been supported by fellowships from the National Endowment for the Arts, the New York Foundation for the Arts, and the Fine Arts Work Center in Provincetown, among others, as well as by residencies at Virginia Center for the Creative Arts, Yaddo, and Djerassi.

After growing up in Los Angeles, Catherine lived in Berkeley, and later in Ohio, Iowa, and Massachusetts before moving to New York, where she worked for *The New York Review of Books.* She left New York to join the faculty of the University of Pittsburgh in 1992 and later returned to California for training and ordination at San Francisco Zen Center's Green Dragon Temple/Green Gulch Farm. She lives again in Pittsburgh, with a garden and a cat.

The headers of *The Gunman and the Carnival* are set in Nanum Myeongjo, a contemporary serif typeface with a warm touch that is part of the Nanum fonts (나눔글꼴) — a set of high quality Unicode fonts designed especially for the Korean-language script "Hangeul" that also support Latin. Designed by Fontrix (폰트릭스,) and published by Naver (네이버).

The body of *The Gunman and the Carnival* is set in Adobe Caslon Pro. The Englishman William Caslon punchcut many roman, italic, and non-Latin typefaces from 1720 until his death in 1766. At that time most types were being imported to England from Dutch sources, so Caslon was influenced by the characteristics of Dutch types. He did, however, achieve a level of craft that enabled his recognition as the first great English punchcutter. Caslon's roman became so popular that it was known as the script of kings, although on the other side of the political spectrum (and the ocean), the Americans used it for their Declaration of Independence in 1776. The original Caslon specimen sheets and punches have long provided a fertile source for the range of types bearing his name. Identifying characteristics of most Caslons include a cap A with a scooped-out apex; a cap C with two full serifs; and in the italic, a swashed lowercase v and w. Caslon's types have achieved legendary status among printers and typographers, and are considered safe, solid, and dependable.

Carol Twombly designed this Caslon revival for Adobe in 1990, after studying Caslon's own specimen sheets from the mid-eighteenth century. This elegant version is quite true to the source, and has been optimized for the demands of digital design and printing.